# I WANTED TO BE A BLUESMAN

*Stories*

## DAVID JOSEPH

## SPECIAL THANKS

As always, special thanks to my incredible cover designer Katarina, my exceptional editor Emma, and my talented layout designer Walt, who work so hard to help me deliver my books into the world. I am inspired by their talent and grateful for their patience. Lastly, to my wife Karen and sons Jackson and Cassius, I simply can't imagine this road without you and thank you for being there every step of the way.

Despite the fact that nearly all the music I listened to originated from the blues, I didn't start with the blues. Far from it. And my love of the blues didn't come from my parents either. My mother listened to show tunes, and my dad liked Burt Bacharach. This isn't meant to be critical of them, but "Raindrops Keep Fallin' on My Head" was never going to get me to Robert Johnson's "Hell Hound on My Trail."

The thing was, all along the way, my musical heroes kept dropping hints. One minute it was Bob Dylan releasing the song "Blind Willie McTell" and the next minute Dylan was referencing Robert Johnson in his Grammy speech. Later he'd compose the song "High Water" and dedicate it to Charley Patton.

At the same time, Led Zeppelin recorded "Traveling Riverside Blues" and Robert Plant and Jimmy Page titled their album *Walking into Clarksdale* in reference to the Mississippi town where Robert Johnson had made his deal with the devil at the Crossroads. Eric Clapton turned Johnson's "Crossroads" into a modern classic, recorded an album with B.B. King, and then played with every blues legend he could find from Muddy Waters to Buddy Guy to John Lee Hooker.

Wherever I turned, it seemed, the blues were there. Robbie Robertson talking about Sonny Boy Williamson or Mick Jagger talking about Sonny Terry. Even if I had tried, there was no escaping the blues. Not in my world, at least. So, I went out and bought Robert Johnson's *King of the Delta Blues*, and I've never looked back.

I've now been listening to the blues for many years, and the songs are just as thrilling and awe-inspiring as the first moment I discovered them. This collection of short stories is, I hope, in some small way, its own tribute to this music that has meant so much to me. And since I can't play guitar like Freddie King or sing like Skip James, I suppose this will have to do.

*David Joseph*

*London 2024*

PS – All stories in this collection were written while listening to the blues. I've included a playlist of some of my favorites for those who may be interested. Apologies to the innumerable amount of absences on this list, as it merely represents a small fraction of the blues tracks I hold dear.

# PLAYLIST

*Cross Road Blues – Robert Johnson*

*Hard Time Killing Floor – Skip James*

*Come Go Home with Me – Lightning Hopkins*

*The Thrill Is Gone – B.B. King*

*Just a Dream (On My Mind) – Big Bill Broonzy*

*Baby Please Don't Go – Big Joe Williams*

*The Waterfront – John Lee Hooker*

*Walk On – Sonny Terry and Brownie McGhee*

*Lady Sings the Blues – Billie Holiday*

*Smokestack Lightning – Howlin' Wolf*

*Death Letter Blues – Son House*

*Nobody Knows You When You're Down and Out – Bessie Smith*

*Mr. McTell Got the Blues – Blind Willie McTell*

*High Water Everywhere, Pt. 1 - Charley Patton*

*You Need Love – Muddy Waters*

*You Got Me Dizzy – Jimmy Reed*

*Thinking My Blues Away – Sonny Boy Williamson*

*I'd Rather See Him Dead — Memphis Minnie*

*See That My Grave Is Kept Clean — Blind Lemon Jefferson*

*Blues at Sunrise — Albert King*

*I Got the Blues Again — T-Bone Walker*

*Nobody's Fault but Mine — Blind Willie Johnson*

*TV Mama — Big Joe Turner*

*It Hurts Me Too — Elmore James*

*Same Old Blues — Freddie King*

*I Can't Quit You Baby — Willie Dixon*

*Riding with the King — B.B. King and Eric Clapton*

*Trust No Man — Ma Rainey*

*Ride with Me Tonight — Honeyboy Edwards*

*Blues for Mama — J. J. Cale*

*Pushin' My Luck — Robert Belfour*

*Blues Don't Lie — Buddy Guy*

*This book is dedicated to all the great musicians who've inspired me by playing the blues. With any luck one day, I'll see you at the Crossroads.*

TABLE OF CONTENTS


I WANTED TO BE A BLUESMAN .............................................................. 1

THE DAY ERIC CLAPTON WALKED IN THE STORE ....................... 14

WHEN MY FIRST WIFE LEFT ME ........................................................ 30

ON A TRIP TO THE MISSISSIPPI DELTA WITH CASPER ................. 44

THE KID WHO LOVED THE BLUES .................................................... 62

AFTER ALL, IT'S NOT BRAIN SURGERY ............................................ 72

THE DEVIL'S MUSIC AND THE SINS OF FATHER MURPHY ........... 82

WHEN BESSIE SMITH CAME TO TOWN ............................................ 94

BRICKLAYING ...................................................................................... 106

RIDING ON A TRAIN IN THE SOUTH ............................................. 118

SEBASTIEN'S LITTLE SISTER ............................................................ 137

ALTON .................................................................................................. 156

ABOUT THE AUTHOR ........................................................................ 189

Every time I woke up after a storm, I thought of my brother. We grew up here, in this little fishing village, where the days are long and people's lives are small. This was the place we were raised, the life we were born into. Dad worked the fishing boats with the men, and Mom taught at the tiny schoolhouse here.

We never left the village, not for anything. There were no trips to the city. No exotic vacations or even dull ones. We shopped at the local market and spent our days and nights in the village. Depending on how you looked at it, we either lived in a detached paradise or an isolated prison. Maybe both. But our contact with the outside world was limited. Dad said we weren't missing anything.

Our one link to the world beyond our small village was the radio, the strange box with frequencies that sat between our beds, with words and music leaking out of it each night as we went to sleep. Looking back today, with all of our fingertip technology, it's impossible to fathom just how important it was to have a radio. Without it, we'd never have heard the news or even known what the voice of the president of the United States sounded like. But what the radio brought us more than anything else was music.

This music we listened to on the radio was different from the music we'd heard in school, the classical music we'd heard in school. There was nothing wrong with classical music, of course, but it didn't speak to us, at least not most of us. And when our teacher placed that needle on a vinyl record in class, we often found ourselves dozing off, lulled to sleep by the syncopated rhythm of the crackling needle, as the record spun.

Listening to music on the radio was just the opposite. It was an awakening, a sonic stimulant, a desperate plea even, and we felt our bodies come to life the moment we heard it. That sound. It was something different. Something new. Something that reflected us, where we were, who we were, how we lived—all without confining us to it. This music was determined and passionate, and it was often played by Black musicians. Today, we'd be told to call them African American, but when we were growing up, they were Black, and we were White.

Sure, there was Sinatra and Bing Cosby and Mel Torme and plenty of White artists. But when we heard Howlin' Wolf or Muddy Waters or Jimmy Reed steamroll over the airwaves, the windows in our bedroom shook, and so did we. This music had teeth. It had guts. It dripped with sweat, and it bled, just like us.

Our parents didn't like the music, this music from the Mississippi Delta or Chicago or other parts of America that were foreign to them, and they didn't particularly like us listening to it. I'm not really sure why, but I'm not going to blame them. Not here and not now. I'm just going to say that they didn't understand it, and nothing we said could explain it to them. Nothing at all, no matter how hard we tried. My brother told me that they'd never get it. At the time, I didn't believe him, but he was right.

Sometimes, as we listened to those throaty voices and heard those squealing guitars, we'd lay in the dark, in our beds, and smile. I couldn't see my brother's face in the dark, but I didn't have to see it to know he was smiling. There was just something so satisfying in the music. And even if the songs were about hardship, pain, and the difficulties life might bring, they filled us with hope, left us with a feeling of possibility, which was something that wasn't easy to come by in our village. You could only get there if you dreamed, really dreamed, and these songs on the radio allowed us to do just that.

Since I knew Mom and Dad weren't fans of the music we listened to, I would try and keep the volume down to a reasonable level out of respect for them. But my brother would reach over from his bed and twist the dial in the opposite direction. He said the music was meant to be played loud, and that it was our duty to play it loud out of respect for the music. Eventually, Mom would yell for us to turn it down and we would, but not until after my brother had attempted to blow the roof off the place, if only for a moment.

I bought my first guitar when I was fifteen. I'd finally scrounged up enough money from cleaning the fishing boats to buy one. It was an acoustic guitar, made from swamp ash wood, and I was determined to learn how to play the blues. My father couldn't believe I had chosen to spend my money on a guitar or, rather, "wasted" my money on it as he put it. Mom said I was free to spend it however I wanted, and my brother just laughed.

"You'll never be able to play that thing," he said. "Not like those guys. And besides, you're not Black."

"We'll see," I said.

Although I wanted to tell him he was wrong about me learning to play, I knew I'd have to prove it. That was the only way, and there was no sense arguing with him. There was never any sense arguing with him, about anything, when he had his mind made up. And he had his mind made up about this. As far as he was concerned, I was a fool.

To be perfectly honest, I wasn't at all sure I could learn to play the guitar either. After all, there were no musicians in our family, and I'd never displayed any type of musical ability. Of course, I wasn't Black either and, if that was a prerequisite for being able to play the blues, well, then I was doomed.

For the time being, though, I just decided to keep quiet. What was the use in arguing? It seemed rather pointless, and I would just have to be patient. Nobody in our house believed in me or was going to support me in this pursuit. So, I checked a book out of the public library on how to play the guitar, and I got to work, learning where to place my fingers on the strings. That's how I did it, and I taught myself. I made sure to learn how to play chords and fingerpick too. Of course, I made tons of mistakes. But one thing I never did was play the guitar when my brother was around. Not ever. He would surely have been merciless, and I wasn't willing to give him the satisfaction.

Somehow, though, I had already learned those songs, those songs we listened to, and they were now embedded in my soul, way down deep, deeper than I even knew. I could remember them word for word, and I could spot the ache in Muddy Water's voice or pick out the wail in B.B. King's guitar. All these sounds had been cataloged in my memory, and I heard them inside my head. I also learned that I had a better ear than I might have thought, and my rhythm wasn't bad either. I just kept playing, practicing, relentlessly, without mentioning it to anyone.

This was around the time my brother was preparing to graduate from high school. Mom and Dad wanted him to go to college if he wasn't going to work on the fishing boats, but he had other ideas. He told us that a friend of his, who was one year older than him, had made it to California.

"He says they're giving away jobs there," my brother told my parents, who clearly disapproved.

It was one thing to dream of making it to Boston or Chicago, as improbable as that was. But California, that was truly beyond the realm of comprehension, not to mention it being well beyond the moral and spiritual realm my parents had existed in for their entire lives.

"How you planning to get to California?" my father snapped one day.

"Bus ticket. Using the money I saved from working on the fishing boats," he said. "Since I didn't waste it on a worthless guitar."

My father looked at me disapprovingly, and I couldn't be sure which one of his sons had disappointed him more. He clearly disapproved of California and everything it stood for, but he was in agreement with my brother's assertion that I had not spent my money wisely.

~ ~ ~

The night before my brother left for California, there was a terrible storm outside. We lay in our room, while the thunder crashed, without saying a word. My brother even let me choose the radio station, and he didn't try and turn it up either. He just sat there in his bed, with his hands behind his head, breathing, pulling the air deep into his lungs and letting it out, while the storm raged outside, and the music played on.

I couldn't pretend that my brother wasn't different, different from me that is. He was, and we rarely saw eye to eye. But he was my big brother, and I still idolized him. We'd shared that bedroom in our small house in this little fishing village all our lives. And we'd fallen asleep listening to the radio together every night for as long as I could remember.

"Wanted you to know that you can keep the radio," he said. "I mean, when I go. It's yours."

"Thanks," I said.

"Sure," he said. "Least I can do, seeing as I'm leaving you here in this boring town."

"Is that why you're leaving?" I asked. "Because you're bored?"

"That and a hundred other reasons," he said. "Haven't you been listening to the songs?"

"What do you mean?" I asked.

"I've got to get out of here," he insisted. "I've got to break free, of this place, this life, of Mom and Dad, all of it. I can't be trapped here, not anymore. It's like Howlin' Wolf said, '*I'm gonna get up in the morning / Hit the Highway 49.*' That's what I've got to do. Hit the highway and head west. I just know it. I can feel it."

We sat quietly a bit longer. I wasn't sure what to say, but I'd never heard my brother talk with so much passion. Oh, we'd listened to the songs together, but I hadn't realized that he'd been building up energy, building up courage, real courage, that the songs had taken him places, places he had to go and could never come back from. Not ever.

"Well, at least you still have your guitar," he said, after a long silence. "Maybe now you'll learn how to play it."

"I know how to play it," I said plainly.

"What are you talking about?" he said. "I've never seen you pick that thing up. Not even once. All it's done is collect dust in that closet."

I slid my feet over the side of my bed and sat up facing my brother without saying a word. I'm not sure why I did it or chose to do it or did it at that moment. Perhaps it was because his remarks had annoyed me, even though he hadn't meant to, not really anyway. Or maybe it was because he was leaving the next morning and I wondered if this might be my last chance. Whatever the reason, I was going to do it.

So, I stood up in the dark and walked across the thick carpet toward the closet. It was pitch-black in the room, but the lights had been out long enough for my eyes to adjust. Besides, I could make my way around our tiny space with my eyes closed, so long as my brother hadn't left anything on the floor.

When I got to the closet, I reached for the doorknob, pulled the heavy, wooden door open, and bent down, in order to reach into the back corner under our hanging clothes. That was where I kept my guitar, and I grabbed it by the neck and walked back over to my bed. I sat down on the edge, with it fastened to my hands like a real bluesman.

"What do you think happens now?" said my brother, laughing. "You think that thing just plays itself?"

I heard him, but not really. I wasn't listening. Not to him. Not anymore. I just sat there, tuning my guitar in the dark. I didn't need a tuner, not as long as I could hear the strings, and I twisted the ends and plucked them until it was perfectly in tune. The radio was still playing, and I waited for the next song to come on, while I got comfortable. I noticed my brother had now sat up and was facing me, but we didn't exchange words.

Just then, the Howlin' Wolf's song "Goin' Back Home" was spun over the airwaves. By now I had gotten good, very good, and I could play along, at least marginally, with any song on the radio by ear. I closed my eyes, took a deep breath and began to play, picking off notes in the dark while the music poured out of the radio and Howlin' Wolf sung:

*Going back home, going back home*

*Got to go home, got to go home*

*Got to go home, got to go home*

*Where I, where I was born*

I just kept playing, with my eyes closed and my head crooked over the guitar, and I noticed my brother had even turned up the radio and was now slapping his knee. I just concentrated on the notes and kept playing until the song ended and the DJ's voice came on over the radio. Afterward I noticed I was out of breath, from the tension I suppose, even though I hadn't sung a word. I set the guitar against the side of my bed and put my head in my hands until I felt my brother reach across and grab my left shoulder with his right hand.

"Well, goddamn," he said. "We got ourselves a bluesman. Blues guitar anyway. We got ourselves a *real* bluesman, a damn White bluesman, but a bluesman nonetheless."

He went on like this for a few minutes, while I smiled in the dark. He couldn't see my face, but I think he knew I was smiling.

"Thanks," I said, before getting up and returning the guitar to the back of our closet.

I walked to the bed and lay on my back again, this time staring at the ceiling. A Jimmy Reed song was playing on the radio now, and I reached over to turn the volume dial back down to a normal level. We both just lay there in our beds, without saying a word for the rest of the night, until we fell asleep alongside one another.

All these years we'd been listening to the radio together each night before bed, discovering this great music, this music from another place, that we weren't going to hear in our town. We felt like explorers, real explorers, who'd discovered something, not so much a new territory, but a secret. A great secret. The music unlocked parts of our being we didn't even know were there.

The songs were powerful. They got inside us, spoke to us, challenged us. They were world-weary and modern all at once, and we were left, each of us, to determine what we were going to do, how we were going to live, to be, now that we had heard those songs.

And yet, while we listened to the same songs, we heard them differently. We brought different parts of ourselves, and parts of ourselves that were different. And where my brother could never stop thinking about Howlin' Wolf telling him to "hit the highway," all I heard was a man who just wanted to "go home."

When I woke up the next morning, the storm had passed. My brother was gone. All these years later, I'm still here.

Buddy Turner owned the record store on 4th Street. When the music industry switched from records to cassette tapes back in the '80s, none of us thought he'd survive, and he almost didn't. Of course, when the industry moved from tapes to CDs, we thought his chances were even less. And Buddy Turner didn't just have any old record store. He had a record store comprised solely of blues and folk records. If ever the adage "adapt or die" was applicable, Buddy's case was it.

He got all kinds of advice, from everyone really, and this was because we liked his record store so much. It was old school, and it oozed charm. Of course, it also played music, and Buddy would spin the records himself. Robert Johnson. Lightnin' Hopkins. Blind Willie McTell. Son House. Howlin' Wolf. Muddy Waters. Sonny Boy Williamson. He had 'em all. B.B. King. Albert King. Bessie Smith, Blind Lemon Jefferson. Jimmy Reed. You name it. To go along with Phil Ochs,

Spider John Koerner. Ramblin' Jack Elliott, Judy Collins, and Peter, Paul and Mary. Bob Dylan of course, at least his folk records. But it was insane, literally insane how much great music he had. Some days, it was worth stopping in just to see what records he was playing.

I could literally spend hours there, leafing through the records, admiring the album covers, wondering just how he could have acquired them all. Of course, some of them, in the early days, came through the labels, but most of these now had been collected, discovered, found, like any other collector only he owned a record shop. But it never felt like a shop. Actually, it felt more like a home with someone's personal record collection, someone's unparalleled record collection if you like that type of music. And I have to say I think Buddy was proud of it. He should have been, since it was pretty spectacular.

There was a time when all the record stores started closing down. That might've seemed like the time for Buddy to make a move, but he decided to stand pat. We told him you never want to be the last one to get out, but Buddy told us that was exactly what he wanted. And he even bought record collections from the stores that were closing. He was either a genius or a fool and, where we saw financial suicide, Buddy saw opportunity. He wanted to be the "last of the Mohicans" and, eventually, he was.

So, how was he able to do it? How was Buddy Turner able to survive all those years and make it through?

Just around the time that the entire world was switching from records to cassette tapes, Buddy told us a story. If the story was true, he was the luckiest record store owner alive. If it was a myth he perpetuated, he was a great businessman. Of course, if it was a lie, that would have made him a liar too. I won't go as far as to say that nobody cared if he was lying, but we wanted it to be true, hoped it was true, and so we played our own roles in sharing the story once we had heard it.

I walked in one afternoon in the mid-'80s. It was cold, brutally cold outside, with the glass frosted over and the wind tearing down the street corridors. To be fair, it was the kind of cold that kept people inside. Winters could be like that here, and people adapted accordingly. You almost had no choice. Even so, I was feeling like I had to get out of my apartment, so I piled on the warmest clothes I had and headed over to Buddy's place to look through some records and shoot the shit with Buddy. It was something to do, and I liked Buddy. I liked Buddy, and I liked his store.

As soon as I walked in the door, I could see Buddy was animated. He hopped down off his stool behind the turntable and raced over to see me. I thought it might have been because Lightnin' Hopkins's "Mojo Hand" was playing. But he was jumpy, really jumpy, which was out of character for him. I mean, Buddy could get excited about the music, but more in a "slow groove" kind of way than the kind where you're gasping for breath.

"You won't believe it," he said, without calming down. "You just won't believe it."

"Believe what?" I said, still trying to get my blood to begin circulating now that I was out of the cold.

"You won't believe who was in here this morning," he said. "That's what."

"Well," I said. "Are you going to tell me?"

"Only if you believe me," he said.

"Sure, I'll believe you," I said. "Why wouldn't I believe you?"

Now, Buddy had musicians stop in before. Once, Mike Seeger (not Pete) stopped in and another time Maria Muldaur came by. So, it wasn't like he'd never had famous people in the place. But he was going seriously mental this time, and I couldn't imagine what (or I should say who) had made such an impression on him that he was literally coming apart before my eyes.

"Well, I've got to tell someone," he said. "And you're the first person I've seen today."

"That hurts," I said. "I thought you were telling me because I was special."

"No," he said. "I'm telling you because you are here! Not that you aren't special, but that's not why I'm telling you."

"Alright," I said. "Well, out with it."

"Eric Patrick Clapton," he said, triumphantly.

"Shut the fuck up," I said. "There's no way Eric Clapton was in this store."

"See!" said Buddy. "I knew you wouldn't believe me."

"Well, I didn't think you were going to say Eric Clapton," I said.

"Well, that's who was here," said Buddy, dead serious.

"The Eric Clapton from Cream?" I asked, now fixing a question.

"The very same one," answered Buddy, proudly.

"Who played in The Yardbirds?" I asked, continuing.

"Who else?" he snapped.

"Slowhand?" I asked, suspiciously but coming around now.

"Yes, yes, yes!" said Buddy.

"How?" I asked, truly dumbfounded. "And why?"

Buddy walked back over to his stool again. He stopped the record that was playing (something he never did before a song ended) and carefully placed another record on the turntable. An ancient recording (at least for this genre) played in the store. "Bad Luck Blues" by Blind Lemon Jefferson.

"He was in town to play a concert last night," said Buddy. "This morning he stopped in, looking for a Blind Lemon Jefferson record."

"Just like that?" I asked.

"Yep," said Buddy. "Just like that."

"What time did he stop in?" I asked, still in shock.

"Just after we opened," said Buddy. "Was my first customer. My only customer this morning, being Monday and all and cold as hell."

"I can't get over this," I said to Buddy, having now finally accepted that Eric Clapton had been there. "Tell me everything. What did he look like?"

"He looked like Eric Clapton," said Buddy. "Had that beard that nearly swallows his face, everything but his eyes, and he was wearing a leather jacket and jeans."

"No shit," I said. "You realize that this is amazing, right? This is fucking amazing."

"I've been trying to tell you," said Buddy.

My mind was racing now. I was trying to think about what I should do, what I wanted to do, and I found myself wanting to tell someone. I mean, after all, we were talking about Eric Clapton. Guitar god Eric Clapton. Blues fan Eric Clapton. Rock icon Eric Clapton.

"From the beginning," I said, almost pleading now.

"So, like I said, I come in and open the store. It's early. It's freezing cold. It's Monday. I turn on the lights, hang up my coat, pour myself a bad cup of coffee. You know, the usual. Nothing odd about it. Typical Monday. Then I picked out my first record of the day."

"What'd you pick?" I asked.

"'Summertime Blues' by Eddie Cochran," said Buddy. "I was trying to be ironic."

"Funny," I said. "So, what happens next?"

"Next thing I know the door opens, and I see this guy walk in," said Buddy. "He looks cold, shivering cold, and he's got his collar up. He takes that deep breath we all take when we come into a warm place from the cold and then politely, half-nods his head upward and says, 'Morning,' with a mannered British accent. I say, 'Hello,' and he just keeps looking through the rows of records, mostly with his back to me. He's quiet and doesn't seem to be interested in making conversation."

"Do you recognize him yet?" I ask.

"No," says Buddy. "Not yet. I mean, he definitely has something familiar about him, but I haven't got a good look at him yet. There's a mysterious quality that I picked up on right away, but no, at this point, I don't have any idea who he is. He's pretty concealed too, with a nice scarf and that thick beard as well."

"So, when do you figure out it's Eric Clapton?" I ask.

"I'll tell you," said Buddy. "You won't believe it. So, he turns and walks straight toward me, while I'm sitting on the stool and the music is playing. Now, I'm looking at him straight in the face, and I know that Eric Clapton is in my store, standing right in front of me, walking toward me even. Eric Clapton! It's all I can do to keep from saying something stupid like, 'You're Eric Clapton,' or even just saying, 'Holy shit,' because that's what I'm thinking. That's exactly what I'm thinking, and I'm sure I wasn't able to disguise this even though I tried to play it cool."

"That couldn't have been easy," I said. "So, how did you try and play it cool?"

"I just said, 'Can I help you find anything?' very professionally, just like he was any other customer who might have stumbled into the store, only now he knew that I knew just by looking at his face, by being face-to-face."

I can hardly believe my ears. Here's Buddy detailing his interaction with Eric Clapton. Just the two of them, in his store, while the blues play and the snow falls outside. It's almost too much to take in, but I can't get the story from Buddy fast enough.

"Well," I said, "what did he say to that?"

"He says, 'Actually, I was wondering if I might be able to use the loo?' which of course is off-limits to customers. Employees only, and there's a sign right here, but he's Eric Clapton, and if he wants to use the loo, he can use the damn loo. I'll tell you that. I certainly wasn't going to tell him he couldn't. Are you kidding me! He's Derek and the Dominos, man. John Mayall and the Bluesbreakers. Right here in my store."

"Sweet Jesus," I say. "He asked you to use the bathroom. I can't believe this."

"So, I tell him it's straight back there and he just nods and says, 'Thanks, mate,' and walks straight back. I mean, he called me mate, like I'm his mate, Eric Clapton's mate. Now, I know that's just an expression if you're from England, but that's what he called me."

"This should be in a movie," I tell him.

"I agree," said Buddy. "That's how I felt, too, like I was in a movie, living in a movie. Of course, nobody else was here, and I thought who will believe me when I tell this story. But you believe me, right? And, in some ways, I guess I was glad that nobody else was here, that it was just me, little ol' me, hanging in the store with Eric Clapton. Me and nobody else. The only word that really fits here is surreal. The whole experience was surreal."

"I bet," I said. "What happened after he came back from the bathroom?"

"After he came out of the bathroom, he spent a few more minutes looking through records before selecting Blind Lemon Jefferson and coming to the front to pay for it. And that's when things got weird."

"Wait," I said. "Are you telling me that things started getting weird now? As if they weren't weird enough already."

"That's what I thought," said Buddy. "But when he's paying for the record, he's acting a little strange and, to be fair, he's pretty shy. In person, I think that's how I would describe him. He wasn't the least bit cocky or arrogant or even all that confident. Yeah, I think I would say he was shy, or at least introverted."

"OK," I said. "That's much better than him being an asshole."

"Absolutely," says Buddy. "No question about it. And then he asks me a question. Asks me if I own the place and I tell him yes. He just acts relieved and says, 'That's good, mate.' I am feeling good about that, so I ask him if he likes the store and he says, 'Of course, mate. It's brilliant, a proper record store.' Now, I'm feeling even better than I was before. After all, here I am talking to Eric Clapton. He's buying a record, and he's telling me that he likes my store. I mean, what's not to be happy about. This is probably the greatest day of my life, for Christ's sake, so I am happy. Damn happy. Couldn't be happier, but then he tells me not to sell the store and I tell him I'm not planning on it. But he's not talking about selling it now. He's talking about ever, and he says that."

"How does he say it?" I ask, now completely transfixed.

"He just says, 'Not ever,' almost as if he's instructing me now, even though it's my store. Now, he is Eric Clapton, so I'm inclined to, if not bow down, at least accept what he's telling me. And so, I nod, but apparently that's not quite good enough for him. Oh, I mean, he's being very nice about it, and he's still shy and humble and very pleasant, but he asks me to promise and he actually says, 'Promise?' waiting for my response. Well, I'd probably promise him my firstborn child at this point, but something tells me I've at least earned the right to ask why, so that's what I ask him: 'Why?' 'You'll have to trust me,' he says, and even though I'd believe anything he told me, I want to know why. It isn't good enough just to trust him, even if I do. I mean, I want to know what's the reason I can never, ever sell this place, no matter the cost. Even if he is Eric Clapton, I figure I have a right to know if I am going to make this solemn promise.

"This is when he looks around to make sure there is no one else there, which is ominous, but also exciting, since he's about to tell me, me and no one else. We've covered a lot of ground in a few minutes with few words and now, apparently, he's going to confide in me, tell me some sort of secret, something that will keep me from ever selling the store."

"Come on," I said. "I can barely stand it."

"I know, I know. I know," says Buddy. "I'm getting there. Well, Clapton, now he just looks at me straight away, like he wants to tell me, like he's got to tell me. 'When I was washing my hands,' he says, 'I looked in the mirror and it wasn't just my face I saw. I saw a ghost,' and I'm thinking he's just hungover or hallucinating or maybe even daydreaming, but he's absolutely convinced, so I ask him who he saw, and he tells me he saw the ghost of Robert Johnson right there, in the mirror. Right here, really. A ghost and not just any ghost. Robert Johnson. King of the Delta blues. Made that deal with the devil at the Crossroads and now apparently his ghost has decided to call my shop home."

"Do you believe in ghosts?" I ask Buddy.

"No," says Buddy. "Or, at least not before this morning. Now, I'm … I'm having second thoughts."

"Because Eric Clapton saw one in your bathroom?" I ask, knowing how judgmental and also insane it sounds.

"Well, yes," says Buddy. "I don't think he would lie, at least not about this."

"Buddy," I said. "I'm not trying to doubt him, but why are you so convinced, aside from the fact that he's Eric Clapton?"

"I get what you're saying," says Buddy. "I really do. But you should have seen him. Clapton, I mean. You just should have seen him when he came out of the bathroom and he was telling me this. He wasn't telling it to me all slick or cool or even demanding. It was more like he was shaken, and he just wanted to be convinced by me that this place would be around. I mean, he was white, I want to say white as a ghost when he came out of the bathroom but that's too much, I know. But he wasn't talking like a man who was lying or trying to play a con. He was talking like a man trying to save his own soul."

"Then what?" I asked.

"Then nothing. Clapton looks satisfied enough that he had my guarantee. He nods appreciatively and extends his hand toward mine. Of course, I grab it enthusiastically and thank him for coming into the store. He just says, 'My pleasure,' and then turns his collar up and walks out into the cold where he just disappears into the distance of the morning."

"Unbelievable," I say, not suggesting I don't believe it. "That's quite a story."

"It would be," says Buddy. "It would be quite a story were it not true. Everything I've told you is true."

"Even the part about your shop being haunted?" I ask for confirmation.

"According to Eric Clapton," says Buddy. "You want a greater authority than that?"

"I suppose you've got me there," I say.

Outside, the wind was blowing so hard that the door rattled without anyone opening or closing it. Buddy had just told me a story nobody would believe if they heard it. And yet, having heard Buddy tell it to me, I had no doubt it was true. It had to be true, but I had no proof. No proof that any of it was true, and yet I was convinced. Somehow, I was convinced. This wasn't like me, since I was logical above all else. And believing in this story defied logic. In fact, it required faith, real faith. Although I wasn't religious, it seemed that somehow faith was what I had seemingly acquired.

From that day on, well, I won't go as far as to say Buddy manipulated the story, but he certainly shared it and so did we. All of us. Buddy's friends. We shared it, and we shared it often. It was a good story after all. A damn good story, an amazing one really. And Buddy certainly profited off it or profited from it, but he definitely profited. The store became the story and the story became the store. People came from all over because of it, and the store surely survived because of it.

From time to time, I allowed a small part of me to wonder if Buddy had made it all up. If he had, it was brilliant. And even if he had, what was Eric Clapton going to do? Respond? Refute it? He'd be better off just keeping quiet and he would probably want the store to survive anyway, being that it was filled from back to front with musical recordings of his own musical idols. Would he have jeopardized that, let all that music be swept away just to set the record straight? Unlikely.

Even though it was possible that Buddy had made the story up, I didn't want to believe he had, so one day I just decided I wouldn't believe he'd made it up, not even for a second. I wouldn't think about that possibility ever again. Not ever. What was the use? What was the point? Cynicism has little value in situations like this one, where faith possessed great value. Since then, I've told everyone I know about the day Eric Clapton came to the store and his insistence that the blues keep on playing, especially on cold winter days, those very coldest of winter days, when the weather decides it's time to even things out and reminds us that sometimes doubt is just a cruel mistress and resistance to what we might see in the mirror is futile.

When my first wife left me, the conventional wisdom was that she had left me for another man, that she had cheated on me, which she had. But that wasn't why she left me. Or perhaps I should say that wasn't why she cheated on me. Maybe there was no difference. And, to be honest, that was easier to explain than the real reason she gave, the reason she gave for cheating on me and leaving me. She left me because she didn't understand me. Or, at least, she no longer understood me. That's what she said, anyway.

The first time she mentioned this we were sitting at a diner on a Sunday morning eating breakfast. When we first met, we went to diners to eat breakfast all the time, so it didn't seem strange (not to me anyway) that we were still eating at diners. After all, diners didn't seem very age-prohibitive. Quite the opposite really, in my opinion. But now we didn't go so often. Almost never, in fact, and I had to wonder why.

From the moment we sat down, I could see she wasn't happy. I could see it right away. Now, I rarely knew why she wasn't happy, but I always knew when something was wrong. That was easy to tell. Still, there didn't seem too much to be unhappy about, getting set to eat together on a Sunday morning, but she had found a way.

"The food is so greasy here," she said.

"If by greasy, you mean good, then you're right," I said, trying to be slightly funny.

"No, I mean greasy," she said, without laughing.

"Well, you used to like greasy food," I said. "In fact, there was a time when they couldn't make the bacon and hash browns greasy enough for you."

"Well, not anymore," she said. "It's unhealthy, and I've outgrown that."

"So is smoking cigarettes," I said. "And you don't seem to have outgrown them."

She burned a hole in my head with her eyes. A waitress rushed past us on the way to another table and dumped two menus in front of us.

"Why did we come here?" she asked resentfully.

"Because they make the best breakfast in town," I said. "That's why."

"It's filled with college kids," she said. "We don't belong here."

"There are more octogenarians here than college kids," I said.

"Well, we aren't them either."

"So, you're telling me we should wait until we are eighty to come back here?" I asked.

"Actually," she said. "I don't ever think we should come back here. Not ever again."

I didn't say a word. I couldn't, really. She was just in a mood, in one of those moods where nothing was going to sit well. So, instead of sending out words to be destroyed, I was the one who sat, in the booth with fake leather, listening to the morning soundtrack of plates clattering next to the bell the cook slapped to let the servers know an order was up. She just sat there, determined to sulk, and ordered a salad, my guess is just so she could bitch about that too. A salad was the only thing you didn't order at a diner, but she had her mind set on being disappointed, so she ordered one.

And that's how it began, the start of her being disappointed, unsatisfied, with me. What was strange was that I hadn't changed, not much anyway. Not much at all. For example, where it might have once seemed charming that I liked diners with character, she now viewed this behavior as sophomoric. And where my lack of desire for fancy clothes or a nice car used to be seen as a sign of my ability not to be materialistic, she now viewed me as grimy and cheap.

She wasn't wrong that there were some ways in which I hadn't evolved. I mean, my constitution was fundamentally the same. The things I used to like I often still liked. I wasn't trying to change these things. Why would I forfeit going to eat at a restaurant I liked simply because I was older, or the patrons were younger? But, somewhere along the line, things had changed for her. Apparently, they had changed dramatically for her, and one day she found herself with an inability to understand the man she had once been happily married to. She didn't even have to say it. I could feel it.

Now, despite this widening gap between us, I didn't think she would seek comfort in the arms of another man. I guess, in that way, I was naive, completely naive, because that was exactly what she did. And Stanton Wells was everything on earth that I was not.

In fact, everyone knew who Stanton Wells was. Everyone in our town that is.

Stanton Wells had been a pretty big deal in the '80s. He was a high school football star turned rock star. I mean, what could be more attractive? His band even had one Top 40 hit, which made all the newspapers here. Plus, he was good-looking. Back in those days he'd been a real ladies' man, one of those guys who wore a leather jacket, rode a motorcycle, and had to fight off hordes of women routinely.

The difference was that, if I had remained consistent, Stanton Wells had become the poster boy for evolution. In fact, all he had done was evolve, and now he was the biggest real estate developer in town. He'd cut his hair, scrapped the bike, put on a suit, and made money hand over fist. He never married or had children, but that didn't stop him from building the biggest house in town. As my wife put it, unlike me, he had made the decision to "grow up" when I had not.

It might appear as if I was jealous of Stanton Wells, but nothing could have been further from the truth. In fact, he repulsed me, and I couldn't understand what she saw in him, I mean, except for the money and the cars and the big house and the looks. But he really was such a tool, the type of arrogant, conceited jackass that made my skin crawl and once upon a time … hers too. However, what he had going for him now was the fact that he was everything I wasn't. That, in and of itself, was appealing to her, probably the most appealing thing of all, in fact.

Still, I didn't see it coming. I never saw it coming. I trusted her, trusted her with my life, and so it was always going to be that way. Even when things started changing, I never suspected she was cheating on me. Maybe we were growing in different directions but cheating … no way. I never gave it a moment's thought, not even when our sex life started waning. I never considered the possibility even for an instant. But I was wrong. I was dead wrong, and I would be the one made to look like a fool.

The one thing that had evolved for me over time was my musical taste. I loved the music of the '60s but, instead of going forward, I just kept going back. I'd always liked the blues but now I found myself immersed (no, obsessed actually) with the Delta blues as far back as the 1920s. Those static-filled recordings by magical guitar players in hotel rooms. Those taut, biting lyrics. And those weary voices that could wail like an electric guitar or croon like a broken heart.

I had given up my CD collection for vinyl records too, and I'd sit there every chance I got, playing record after record, listening to the blues.

Now, my wife, she was pretty open-minded when it came to music. She liked rock and pop, R&B, country, Motown, and even listened to a fair amount of hip-hop and rap. Jazz put her to sleep, although she didn't mind it. But she drew the line at the blues.

I was in my study at home listening to Charley Patton one evening when she peeked her head in for no other reason than to pick a fight with me. Now, she would later say that all she was doing was trying to "understand" me, but if you are "trying" to understand someone, I believe you are required to do a particular amount of "trying," which she clearly held little interest for her.

Anyway, she gazes into the room unassumingly and inquires, "Who are you listening to?"

"Charley Patton," I say.

"Never heard of him," she says, even though I'd been listening to him for years.

"He's a bluesman from the South," I say, playing along. "In fact, he's referred to as the father of the Delta blues."

"They all sound the same to me," she says in a dismissive manner that is also racist, even if it's not meant to be.

"His sound is very distinct," I say. "But he did influence lots of other artists."

"Like who?" she asks, wondering if she knows any of them.

"Well," I say. "Robert Johnson for one. Howlin' Wolf too."

"Robert Johnson," she says. "I've heard of him. Is he the one who met the devil?"

"The very one," I say, slightly impressed, even if she'd heard me tell the story a dozen times. "He was also poisoned to death by a jealous husband."

"That so?" she says. "Jealous of what? He must have done something bad."

"Supposedly, he was just flirting," I say. "In those days, that was enough?"

My wife doesn't say anything. At the time, I think maybe she's just contemplating the death of Robert Johnson. But, looking back, maybe she's thinking about us, since she's already having an affair with Stanton Wells. But she knows I'm not going to poison anyone. That's for sure. She knows that. Still, perhaps this gave her pause, and perhaps she was wondering if I knew about Stanton—which I did not at the time.

"Why do you listen to these guys?" she says, changing the subject. "Charley Patton? Robert Johnson? Howlin' Wolf?"

"Why?" I ask, repeating the question.

"Yes," she says calmly. "Why?"

"I love the blues," I say. "And they are remarkable artists?"

"They don't sound remarkable to me," she says. "Unless you mean because they can't sing."

This is the second shot she's thrown, in earnest, across the bow. Usually she'd come out more overtly, but tonight she's taking a more nuanced, sophisticated approach. She's getting the digs in when I least expect, mixed in between feigned interest in actually having a conversation. I need to be on my toes, and I can't let myself be duped or she'll eat me alive.

"You don't think he's a great singer?" I ask, keeping my cool.

"He's awful," she says.

"You don't hear the raw aching in his voice?"

"No," she says. "I'm doing the aching listening to him."

"Do you hear the power, complete with that classic bluesman's growl we often hear today?"

"It definitely sounds like growling," she laughs. "That's a good description."

I decide to continue on, answering her question to the best of my ability.

"He's also an excellent guitar player," I remark.

"What makes him excellent?" she asks, just questioning my knowledge now.

"Well, he could play all kinds of music," I say. "He was also innovative. Some say he was one of the first players to use a guitar slap and he had great rhythm as well."

"Sounds ordinary to me," she says. "And ancient."

"He was born in 1891," I say.

"Like I said, ancient," she remarks.

"He was anything but ordinary," I say. "Could even play between his legs or behind his back."

"Is that right?" she says, doubtfully.

"Sure is," I say proudly, before adding what is only probable speculation. "Influenced Jimi Hendrix."

"That can't be true," she says.

"Why's that?" I say.

"How could this guy influence Jimi Hendrix?"

"Believe it," I say, feeling I have earned a point.

"I don't," she says matter-of-factly.

It wasn't like this when we'd first gotten married. It was nothing like this. I can't say she liked the blues when we first got married. That probably isn't true. But she didn't seem annoyed that I liked the blues. That was never apparent. Now, perhaps that was just because our relationship was new. After all, people tolerate all kinds of things when a relationship is new, when they don't want to offend the other person for fear it will jeopardize things. But all of that falls away in time, and she had no fear of offending me now. Maybe it was better that she was being honest with me, but I have to say I preferred it when she was more tolerant, more respectful, more unlikely to offend. Now, it just seemed like she had grown impatient, resentful almost, of everything I was. From my attire to my choice of restaurant right down to the Delta blues, there was nothing about me, it seemed, that didn't annoy her. Now, when it came to my clothes or my car or the diner even, I had merely become saddened by these changes. However, when it came to the blues, I was offended. I was downright offended. And I felt a need to defend the blues, to stand up for Charley

Patton. Sure, come at my inadequacies as much as you'd like, I thought to myself. But stay away from Charley Patton, the great Charley Patton. I took that affront very personally.

"He also wrote some great songs," I say.

"Name one," she says.

"'High Water,'" I say.

"Never heard of it," she says.

"Funny," I say. "Since it's about a flood, a terrible flood, with high water all around. Sort of like our marriage."

"Well then," she says. "I guess you would think I'd have heard of it, what with the water we've taken on."

"Listen," I say. "I'm sorry. I'm just angry, I suppose. Or maybe I just can't understand why, why … you're so angry with me."

"I'm not angry with you," she says, coldly. "I just don't like the blues."

"That's alright," I say, more understanding now. "You don't have to like them."

"What then?" she says. "What's the problem then?"

"It's not that you don't like them," I say. "It's that you don't want me liking them."

"That's not exactly true," she says. "Not exactly. It's not that I resent you liking them so much as I don't understand it."

"What don't you understand?" I ask. "You hear the blues, right?"

"I hear music," she says. "Or noise, rather. I hear some kind of noise, but it doesn't move me."

"Do you hear the pain in that 'noise' as you put it?" I say. "It's such a raw expression of emotion."

"Not to me," she says. "To me, it's just a racket. It's an awful racket. Moreover, I can't stand to listen to it, and I can't stand to hear it."

There it was. It had taken a while, but we had gotten there. We had finally gotten there, arrived, after all these years and all these words and all these dialogues. We had finally arrived, and it was good to feel as if we were there, finally there, at a place where we were being truthful, completely truthful, with one another. The unassailable, unavoidable, unenviable truth.

"Well," I say, "If you can't hear the blues. If you can't even stand to listen to the blues, to these great blues musicians, when they are pouring their hearts out to you, how can I ever expect you to listen to me?"

"I don't know," she said. "I just don't know. Of course, I hear you. I really do, but I suppose I've stopped listening."

I headed to the Mississippi Delta with Casper. Can you believe that? Casper! His parents named him Casper, like the ghost, which might not have been such a dumb idea, since Casper was white. Lily white. Man, he was as white as it fucking got. Anyway, I headed south with Casper in his old Buick.

It was a pretty long drive to Mississippi, but it was nothing we couldn't handle. After all, we'd been across the country to the West Coast, so heading to the South from New York City didn't seem like that big a deal. Still, it was a long drive, and we planned to take our time and do it in three days.

All this started one afternoon when Casper and I were talking about what it takes to be great … at anything, really. At a job. A sport. Academic subject. Family life. Music. Art. Just the idea of greatness in and of itself and what it takes if someone dares to achieve it.

That was when Casper said that he thought you had to sell your soul to be truly great at anything.

"You mean like Robert Johnson?" I said.

"The guitar player?" he asked.

"Yes," I said. "That's the one."

"Did he sell his soul?" asked Casper.

"Literally," I said. "Legend says he sold his soul to the devil at the Crossroads and that's how he gained his otherworldly guitar talent."

"Is that right?" asked Casper.

"That's what the legend says," I told him. "If you believe it."

"Sounds far-fetched to me," said Casper.

"Why's that?" I asked. "You are the one who suggested soul-selling is required to achieve greatness."

"Not to the devil," Casper corrected me.

"Why does it matter who you sell your soul to?" I asked. "That doesn't seem all that important."

"Did it matter for Robert Johnson?" asked Casper.

"Well, they say he was poisoned by the husband of a woman he flirted with," I said.

"That's certainly a bit of bad luck," said Casper. "A heavy price for selling his soul to the devil, I suppose."

"Yes," I admitted. "But then again, he was one of the greatest guitarists of all time."

"You're suggesting it may have been worth it?" asked Casper.

"Well, it was certainly worth it for us," I said. "Look at the great music he gave us. We're still listening today."

"I imagine he didn't know that would be the case," said Casper.

"No," I said. "That's true. But I think he knew he was great, truly great, that his long fingers had received a special gift, an otherworldly gift."

"Maybe that was enough," said Casper.

And that's how this trip came to be. This improbable trip in an old Buick, traveling from New York City to Clarksdale, Mississippi, in the middle of the summer when the temperatures were soaring, and you could sweat through your T-shirt walking to your car. That's how it all began for us, with a simple conversation about Robert Johnson, king of the Delta blues.

I knew quite a bit about the blues. Or, I should say I'd learned quite a bit about the blues. I worked to learn about the blues, since they seemed like such an important influence on the artists I liked best, whether it was Bob Dylan or The Band or The Rolling Stones. The one constant was the blues, I suppose. The blues were always there, lurking, imposing, adding texture and grit beneath the surface. No matter where you went, it seemed, the blues were never far away. Heck, even Bob Dylan's first professional gig was opening for John Lee Hooker at Gerde's Folk City in 1961.

Now, Casper, he didn't know much about the blues, which I thought was funny, since he liked country music. There were country blues of course, and country, at its core, was inextricably linked to the blues. That being said, his education took him back as far as Hank Williams, and that was about it. That was far enough for him, and so he didn't know much about Delta blues musicians plying their trade in the 1920s and '30s, which was fine. But he liked music. He liked it a lot, and he seemed happy enough to learn more.

So, it was summer, and everyone was heading to the beaches on the East Coast, all our friends anyway. That's where they headed, young people, when the weather improved and the sun shone and the clothes came off. But I didn't belong at the beach. Heck, I didn't even know how to swim. And Casper, well, he had no business being at the beach with his skin. He'd just fry like bacon in a matter of minutes. Anyway, one evening we were drinking whiskey at a bar in the city, with sirens outside and people all around, when the idea came to Casper.

"Let's go to Clarksdale," he said. "This summer. Let's go to Clarksdale."

Now Clarksdale is not exactly a vacation destination. In fact, it was a place that had been beaten down, where nearly half the people lived below the poverty line. But we'd been drinking a lot, and so I figured maybe it was the alcohol talking.

"Clarksdale's not exactly Myrtle Beach," I said. "Or even the Jersey Shore."

"But it is the place with the Crossroads," he said. "The place where Robert Johnson sold his soul to the devil."

"That's true," I said. "You've been doing your research."

"So, you up for it?" he asked. "A road trip to Clarksdale, Mississippi."

"I've never been to Mississippi," I said, trying to convince myself this was a good idea.

"Then it's settled," declared Casper. "We're going to Clarksdale."

"Wait," I said. "I haven't agreed to anything."

"Oh, come on," said Casper. "You don't have anything better to do."

Much as I wanted to disagree with him, he was right. I didn't have anything better to do, and Clarksdale was an intriguing place to think about visiting. Run-down. Depressed. Dirty. Hot and humid, but dripping in history. Blues history. Casper could tell I was going to agree to his idea. I was a pushover, and he knew that, even if I pretended to need convincing. Just then, Cathy, a friend of ours, walked over.

"You boys coming to the beach with us this summer?" she asked as if she had been listening to our conversation.

"Nope," said Casper triumphantly. "We're going to Clarksdale."

"Clarksdale?" asked Cathy. "Where's that?"

"Mississippi," I said.

"Why are you going there?" asked Cathy.

"To see where Robert Johnson sold his soul to the devil," said Casper. "Want to come?"

"No thanks," said Cathy. "You guys are weird."

She walked back over to her friends at a nearby table. I could tell Casper was feeling good about himself. He always felt good about himself when he wasn't following the crowd, when he wasn't trying to compete with anyone, when he was zigging while others were zagging. And taking a trip to Clarksdale made him feel good. After all, nobody we knew was going to Clarksdale.

"Hey," Casper said, as if just coming up with the idea. "We could stop in Nashville on the way."

"Aah, now I get it," I said.

"Get what?" said Casper. "What are you implying?"

"Saying we should go to Clarksdale was just a way for you to get us to Nashville."

"You think so little of me," said Casper, sarcastically.

"Not at all," I said. "I just know you."

"What's that supposed to mean?" he snapped.

"It means I know you're clever," I said. "And that you see all the angles."

"Well," said Casper. "It would be cool to see the Grand Ole Opry too. I mean, in addition to the Crossroads."

"Yes," I agreed. "It would be cool."

~ ~ ~

We should have turned our car right around, taken it as a bad omen and headed back to the city, when our air-conditioning let go in Northern Virginia. But we were still blessed with the foolishness of youth, and we just kept going. By the time we crossed into Tennessee, we felt like we were going to expire. It wasn't just hot. It was humid. Crazy humid. Hallucination humid.

We whipped by the trees on the interstate, trees that were getting greener and taller it seemed as we headed south, and you could see the heat. It's one thing to feel the heat, to physically experience the humidity, but it seemed like we could see it with our own eyes, out in the air, almost as if the trees themselves were dripping with perspiration. Perhaps we were hallucinating after all. Either way, by the time we saw signs for Nashville, we had to get out of that car.

It felt like we hadn't spoken in hours, not because we were angry with one another, but because we were just exhausted, beaten down by the heat. We pulled into the parking lot of a cheap motel on the outskirts of the city and said we'd stay there for a night. We ended up staying for five.

Sure, there were plenty of things to do in Nashville, what with the Grand Ole Opry, the Ryman Auditorium, and my personal favorite, the Jack Daniels Distillery. But we didn't stay for any of those things. No, we stayed there because of Scarlet.

Casper was the kind of guy who never fell, not really hard, for a woman. But he sure fell for Scarlet. He'd met her on our first night in town, not at a bar or restaurant but at a filling station. They call them gas stations everywhere else, but in the South they call them filling stations, so that's what I'll call them here. But there he was, just using the gas pump when a young woman was across from him pumping her own gas. Now, Casper, he'd talk to anyone, so it was no surprise he struck up a conversation.

"Hi," he said. "Can I help you?"

"You don't work here," she said, looking him up and down. "You think I can't pump my own gas?"

"I … I … I'm sure you can, ma'am," he stumbled. "I was only trying to be helpful."

"No, you weren't," she laughed. "You were trying to pick me up."

"Well," said Casper with his head staring down shyly. "Maybe just a little bit."

She walked back around to the other side of her car, opened the door, and bent over, reaching for something inside, while Casper watched as he was pumping our gas. Moments later, she returned with a piece of paper that had a phone number written down on it.

"I am staying at the Red Lion," she said. "This is my number if you want to get a drink."

"Yes. Great. Of course. Yes. I'd love to," Casper stammered again.

"OK," she laughed. "I'm convinced."

Then she got in her car and drove off. I am not sure why, but this was the second time on our trip when I felt like we should have turned around and headed back to New York. It was just a feeling, but I felt it. There was just something about her, something like an omen that felt eerily similar to that moment days earlier when the air-conditioning had dropped out of our car. Not surprisingly, Casper didn't sense this at all, but I think that's only because he was too busy thinking about Scarlet.

Scarlet was a very beautiful woman. She had brown skin and freckles. You didn't see many women with brown skin and freckles, but she had them. She had full, red lips that stood out against her skin, frizzy hair, and sparkling green eyes. Her figure was striking too, curvy, with legs that were poured into her pair of jeans. That's what she wore, too. Jeans. Blue jeans and a white T-shirt.

Immense beauty wrapped in an outfit with no frills. No frills at all.

"Be careful," I said, when Casper got back into the car.

"Of what?" he said. "Of her? Come on."

"I'm serious," I said. "Be careful."

"You're just jealous," said Casper. "That's all."

"Maybe," I said, not disagreeing with him. "Maybe."

We went to the motel, unpacked our bags, and plopped down on our beds. I put the TV on, while we sat numbly watching an old episode of *NCIS* that seemed as good as anything else. I was resting my eyes for a second, when Casper decided to speak.

"I'm gonna call her," he said. "I think I'm gonna call her right now."

"Good idea," I said. "That way you won't look overeager, since you met her an hour ago."

"You'll see, smart ass," said Casper. "She might be leaving tomorrow."

I didn't say anything. Of course, he was right, and of course I was jealous, at least a little bit, of a woman like that. But I was also worried, a tad worried. More than a tad, really. She'd taken an unusual interest in Casper, it seemed, and been pretty forward with him as well. In my experience, when things appeared too good to be true, they often were, and this seemed like it might be one of those instances. But Casper was in love. Love at first sight that is, or at least as close as anyone can be to love at first sight. And nothing I could say to him was going to keep him from finding out.

We met Scarlet at a bar close to her motel. She had freshened up and put on a touch of makeup, but she still wore very low-maintenance clothes, which was just the opposite of the women we knew back in the city. But she was beautiful. There was no question about that.

We sat with her at a high-top table, just the three of us. It was quickly apparent that Scarlet was smart too. Very smart. And more than smart, perceptive, and perceptive in a way that can only be derived from experience, from life that had already been lived.

"So," she said, ready to start asking questions. "Where y'all from? 'Cause I know you ain't from around here."

Casper was starstruck, so I answered.

"New York," I said. "New York City."

"You're a long way from home, fellas," she said. "What brought you here? Opry? On your way to Graceland to see Elvis?"

"Actually, we're headed to the Crossroads," I said, while Casper looked on dreamily. "We want to see where Robert Johnson made his deal with the devil."

"Is that right?" she said, appearing slightly more impressed than if we were heading to see Elvis. "Hmm."

"That's right," I said.

"Sure is," said Casper.

Scarlet laughed. She laughed in a genuine way, a completely genuine way, like she was charmed by us, amused. And I could only imagine that she had found us to be the ultimate marks in some kind of scheme she was planning or simply a breath of fresh air and an escape from her real life, whatever that was. Wherever that was.

"What about you?" I asked.

"From New Orleans," she said. "I'm creole."

"Do you like the blues?" asked Casper awkwardly.

"Honey, I'm from New Orleans," she said. "Sure, I like the blues, but I'm more of a jazz woman myself. New Orleans and all."

"Lonnie Johnson's from New Orleans," I said.

"Oh yeah," she said. "There are quite a few bluesmen from the Bayou. Professor Longhair. Slim Harpo too."

"I'm impressed," I said.

"Me too," said Casper.

"But it's jazz that flows through the city today. Jazz runs through our veins. After all, the blues headed north, if I am being honest, years ago."

"So, what are you doing in Nashville?" I asked.

"Running," said Scarlet in a plainspoken way that didn't reveal whether she was being truthful or messing with us.

"From who?" perked up Casper.

"My husband," she said, smiling now. "He's six-foot-five."

"Let's go," I joked, looking at Casper.

"Who's joking?" said Scarlet still smiling. "Do you think I'm joking?"

"Come on, man," said Casper. "She's joking."

"Is she?" I asked.

"You'll have to figure that out," said Scarlet. "Decide for yourselves. Know what I mean?"

"Well, I believe her," I said. "And I'm afraid of being right."

"Don't worry," said Casper. "You're not right."

"Aw, sugar," said Scarlet. "You're very sweet."

Scarlet took her hand and placed it on the side of Casper's face. She looked at him rather sweetly and then leaned in and kissed him across the table. That was my cue to leave and, despite my feeling that Casper was making a mistake, I had to let him make it. Or at least I couldn't stop him from making it. So, I went. That's what I did. I left that bar and went back to the motel and turned on the TV, where *NCIS* was still playing.

I spent the next four days on my own in Nashville. The town was alright. Actually, it was nice. It just wasn't why I'd come on this trip, and yet here I was, touring the city, listening to country music, and sitting in the motel ordering in food while *NCIS* played on repeat. Not exactly the Mississippi Delta, but spending so much time in the hotel room did make me think about Robert Johnson. It made me think about his blues and also that he recorded in hotel room 414 at the Gunter Hotel in San Antonio. Twenty-nine songs. Twenty-nine indelible songs. Songs that survived time. That was all the music that Robert Johnson had time to leave us with, done by the age of twenty-seven, not much older than we were.

According to Casper, he and Scarlet spent the next four days in bed, in her bed. Predominantly naked, their bodies wrapped around one another in her hotel room, breaking only to sleep, shower, and have food delivered. Apparently, she was an extraordinary lover, and Casper continues to call these four days the best four days of his life.

On what turned out to be their last day together, they were having sex in her hotel room when the door burst open, when the door was busted down, leaving Scarlet's six-foot-five husband standing in the doorway. He was brandishing a gun, a Colt 45, and he was as terrifying as one might have imagined.

"Keep going, boy," he directed Casper, tipping his gun in his direction. "You won't mind if I watch you fuck my wife, will you?"

"Don't do this," screamed Scarlet, still underneath Casper. "Let him go."

"Not sure you're in a position to make demands," scowled her husband. "You heard me, boy. Keep going."

What happened next isn't perfectly clear but, apparently, Casper kept going, kept fucking, fucking for his life it seemed, if ever there was such a thing. The last thing he remembers was the sound of the gun ringing out, two shots that her husband unloaded into his ass.

Right into his ass, from six feet away, while he was fucking Scarlet. Casper passed out from the pain, which he could only describe to me as "burning a hole" in his ass. The next thing he remembers is waking up in the hospital.

Fortunately, for him, and for Scarlet, someone had seen a man with a gun outside the motel. The police had arrived just as her husband was emptying the gun. He was taken into custody, and Casper was taken to the hospital. Scarlet gave her statement to the police, and we never saw her again. After his surgery to remove the bullets, Casper tried to contact her by phone, but the number was no longer in service, and that was that. She had taken off, made a clean break. Her husband was in jail, and she was gone.

When Casper was let out of the hospital, we headed back to New York City. He felt bad that we had never made it to the Crossroads, to Robert Johnson's Crossroads, but not as bad as his ass felt sitting in that car, with no air conditioning, for nearly twenty hours on the drive back to New York.

But the ride did give me time, time to think, about what we'd been through and about how this whole trip came about in the first place. It all started with that question about selling your soul, the way Robert Johnson sold his to the devil down at the Crossroads. And I had to wonder. Had Casper sold his soul to be with Scarlet? Had Scarlet sold hers for her freedom? Did we all sell our souls at some point in our lives, for something we wanted so much we were willing to sacrifice everything? And if so, was it worth it? That was really the question in the end. The only question that mattered. Was it worth it?

As we cruised through Pennsylvania and New Jersey, into New York State, and across the Hudson River, I thought about Robert Johnson, how he'd managed to make it to the Crossroads when I had not. Although he'd left us at twenty-seven, he'd left us with an awful lot. He'd made that deal, and he'd lived with the consequences. Died with them too. In its own way, it wasn't selfish. It was admirable, and I wondered if I'd be able to do the same.

We played music in the restaurant kitchen all the time. Tried to rotate it. You know, something for everyone. That kind of thing.

It wasn't a gourmet place by any stretch, more like a greasy spoon, but a good greasy spoon and a hardworking one at that. We had a pretty good customer base, you know, so there was never a dull moment.

Most of the people in the kitchen chose R&B, hip-hop, or some radio pop. A couple chose rock music, and we had an old guy who liked Motown. But there was this one kid, young kid, maybe nineteen or so and a damn good grill man. Now, he was interesting. Most of the time he worked at a pretty slow pace. He was mellow, really chill, and everybody liked that about him. All except for the fact that there were times when we needed him to pick up the pace. That's how it is at a joint like this, one that makes good burgers and fries and Reuben sandwiches. One minute, you'll be moving along at a relaxed pace and the next you'll have twenty burgers to cook all at once.

This usually happened when the restaurant got busy but, occasionally, one person would arrive and place a huge order—sometimes to go and other times when a group or a team would stop in. At those times, we were really overmatched, and we had to make every second count. The kid wasn't used to making every second count. He was a good worker, but hurrying was not his style, and he had a tendency to get irritated any time the boss urged him to get a move on it.

The lone exception to this was when the blues were playing. I mean, if Muddy Waters or Albert King or Big Joe Turner were playing, this kid could move, really move, which was funny since the blues are rarely played at a fast pace. But it didn't matter. If this kid heard the blues, his whole body started shaking. His feet started shimmying, and he became the fastest grill man you'd ever seen in your life. I mean, he'd line 'em up, the patties, right in a row, and cook a slew all at once. He'd turn the heat up and down to keep from burning the meat, and sometimes he'd even flip them in the air, high in the air, if he heard a great lick on the guitar. None of us had ever seen anything like it, and we couldn't help but be impressed. Damn impressed.

The trouble was that nobody else in our kitchen was a big fan of the blues. Everyone got their choice of music, but the kid's music played more often than any of ours because it was our "go-to" anytime the crowds poured in, and the orders built up. Some of the staff didn't think that seemed fair, and it probably wasn't. But we weren't playing the blues because it was fair. We were playing the blues because it was the only way he'd move his ass when we needed everyone working with a sense of urgency, a real sense of urgency.

The manager, well, he didn't give a crap about what was fair—at least not what was fair to us. He was focused on what was fair to the customers, and if we didn't like the blues playing more than other genres, we could find another place to work. It was as simple as that.

Now the kid, he didn't say a word either way. He didn't ask for the blues to be played. Nor did he complain when they were not. He wasn't motivated by the manager's pleas to move quicker when other music was playing, and he seemed like he would have simply moved on had he been given an ultimatum. In fact, he was fairly indifferent to all of us. He was perfectly pleasant, but he was indifferent, at least that's how he acted.

Some people saw this as arrogance, but I never saw it that way. Not at all. He was simply as mellow and unaffected about this as anything else. Almost like he didn't have a choice, like he didn't have free will, like the music dictated his pace. He was just there, along for the ride, doing his thing, whether quickly or slowly. That idea, that he had given himself over to the music like some kind of higher power, well, it rubbed some folks the wrong way. But he wasn't going to change, and he wasn't going to be bothered either. And there was something enviable about that.

One afternoon, I happened to be needed on the grill. Now, I was normally on the register. That was my real forte, punching keys. I wasn't much of a grill man, but I'd wanted to ask him some things for a while, so I was perfectly happy to be stationed there.

"Hey, kid, how ya doing?" I said, just trying to make conversation.

"I'm alright, man," he said.

"That's good," I said. "That's good. Glad to hear it."

"Cool," he said.

"Listen," I said. "Can I ask you something?"

"Sure," he said. "People are always going to ask you something or tell you something when they start a sentence with 'Listen.'"

I laughed, but I was thinking he was probably more intelligent than I'd given him credit for.

"Well," I said. "That's probably true."

"Just fucking with you, man," he said. "We're cool. I'm just chillin'."

"So," I said. "You like the blues."

"I do," he said.

"And you always choose the blues when it's your turn to choose," I said.

"That's right," he said.

He was a quiet kid. Naturally quiet. He would answer when spoken to, but he wasn't verbose. That was for sure. He was economical with his words, really, and he said about as little as he needed to.

"I'm not trying to pry. Really, I'm not," I said. "But can you tell me why you always choose the blues?"

"You really want to know?" he asked.

"I do," I said.

"How old are you," he asked.

"Me?" I asked pointing at myself. "You want to know how old I am?"

"Yes," he said.

"I … I'm forty-seven," I said, without embarrassment but wondering the significance.

"Do you like the blues?" he asked.

"I do," I said. "But I only listen to them at certain times."

"Figured," he said, not so much smugly, but like he had foreseen this answer.

"What does that mean?" I asked, a little defensive.

"At night?" he asked. "You listen at night?"

"Yes," I said. "Usually."

"When the sky is dark, maybe after the kids have gone to bed?" he asked.

"Yes," I asked.

"With a whiskey in your hand, perhaps?" he asked.

"What's this have to do with anything?" I asked.

"I'm getting there," he said.

It was interesting. He was constructing his answers in much the same way he worked the grill. Calm. Eerily calm. Composed. Almost methodical. If I wasn't on the receiving end, I would have said it was impressive. As it was, it felt slightly uncomfortable. He was young, yes, but he was wise too. Moreover, he seemed to be unfazed, completely unfazed, by my initial question.

"Go on," I said. "I'm listening."

"You probably listen to the blues when you're sad, when you're down, maybe just tired or worn out, exhausted from the day," he suggested. "Yes?"

"That may be true," I conceded.

"And the blues are often a little downbeat. Yes?" he said and then expounded on his idea before I could answer. "Perhaps downbeat is the wrong word, but blues songs are often about loss, hard times, pain and suffering. When you say to someone that you've got the blues, that by nature speaks to being down. True?"

"I think I'd agree with that," I said.

We were continuing this conversation after an order had come in for a cheeseburger, and we were working the grill as we went back and forth. Actually, he was working the grill. I was mostly watching him work the grill, which was fine by me. Beyond knowing more than I did about the blues, he was a better cook than I was too. He scraped up the burger without getting it stuck to the grill and then casually tossed a piece of cheese on top, almost like a frisbee. It landed perfectly and needed no adjustment with his fingers. Once the cheese had melted, he slid the spatula underneath and relocated the patty on the bun that was open on the plate with fries. Then he slid it out onto the shelf and called out to let the server know it was ready.

"This is the thing," he continued. "The most important thing of all."

"I'm all ears," I said.

"It's so simple, really," he said. "Which, I think, is why people don't recognize it."

"OK," I said, awaiting some sage wisdom.

"It's ironic," he said.

"What's ironic?" I asked, not following him.

"It's ironic that all these sad songs, all these *blue* notes, all these repetitions, these mournful tales of loss … well, they make us feel better."

"What does?" I asked, trying to understand.

"The blues come from pain, but they don't make us feel sad," he said. "They aren't soul sucking. They're life affirming. That's what makes them special."

"I suppose so," I said. "I'd never thought of them that way."

"Most people don't," he said. "That's why they pull out the whiskey on the porch. But they do feel better after listening, and it's not because of the whiskey."

Damn kid had a point. He had a good point, a damn good point. The blues don't make us feel bad. Despite the origin of the songs, we feel better, better about ourselves, better about our lives, better about life in general, after listening to them. Goddamn. That's a pretty neat trick, I thought—although I had to admit I was a tad embarrassed it took a nineteen-year-old to show me.

"Fuck me," I whispered under my breath to him.

"See?" he said. "I told you."

"So," I said. "That's why you cook like gangbusters when the blues are playing?"

"Of course?" he said. "It's not like I have a choice, man."

"Everyone has a choice," I said.

"That's where you're wrong," he said. "We don't choose how we feel about something."

"True," I said. "But we choose how we respond to those feelings."

"You've got it backward," he said. "We don't choose how we respond. The feelings choose for us, at least if we're being honest."

"Are you saying I'm not honest," I asked, taking offense.

"I'm saying that you should listen to the blues, man," he said. "Just listen. That's all. All you need to do. It's the fucking blues, man. They'll do the rest."

He shook his head, like he was exhausted from our conversation. Not angry. Just tired. He'd grown weary of explaining, and he turned his attention back to the grill, where he was fixing a grilled cheese with bacon. It was his turn, and he'd chosen John Lee Hooker's "It Serves You Right to Suffer." He was right. He was goddamn right. I did deserve to suffer. And the blues played on.

I loved cars, but I'd never been able to buy myself a new one, which was alright. You do what you can, live the way you're able, and get on with it. That's all you can do, really. All any of us can do. Get on with it and keep getting on with it. Until we can't, that is.

Up until that point, I'd driven just about everything you could imagine. Chevy Malibu. Buick LeSabre. Silverado pickup truck. Even a broken-down, old Eldorado. Fucking hell. For a time, I even rocked a Plymouth Neon. I mean, I drove 'em all, and I wasn't going to be choosy. Shit, I wasn't in a position to be choosy.

It all stemmed from that one decision I'd made years ago, when I was deciding whether to be a brain surgeon or a janitor. You know, I'd thought it over for quite some time, evaluated all the pluses and minuses, sought the appropriate counsel, and ultimately listened to my heart. In the end, janitor was just a better fit for me. Fuck me.

Funny thing is, if you asked most people, that's basically what they'd think, that I had a choice of being a brain surgeon or a janitor, rich or poor, successful or not, that it's all just a matter of priorities. That simple. Land of the free and all. Land of opportunity. Holy hell. Anyone who tells you that, who really believes that, was given an opportunity from the start. Me, I had to earn my way up to janitor. Head janitor, actually.

Look, I'd started out boosting cars. That's how it all began. Actually, I didn't start out boosting cars. Jimmy King did. But we were friends, and it wasn't long before I was boosting cars too. This ain't no excuse, not at all, but we weren't the first poor kids to steal cars. It's what poor kids did, at least the ones I knew. Not all of them worked their way up, pulled up their bootstraps, that sort of thing. Shit, our bootstraps were already pulled up. For as long as we could remember, we were doing whatever we could to bring home money and help the family. That was the reality of it, and everything was a means to an end, really.

Even so, I was scared shitless the first time I stole a car with Jimmy. Now, Jimmy, he'd done this dozens of times before, so he wasn't all that nervous. Or, at least he didn't seem all that nervous. Not like me, anyway.

And look, we weren't really stealing that car, that first car. We were basically just starting it and moving it to another location. But it wasn't ours to move, and we were hot-wiring it. Jimmy knew cars, and he picked an easy car to hot-wire for my first time. It was an Oldsmobile Cutlass, and it was easier than I thought.

The most important thing, according to Jimmy, was not to panic. That didn't help you move any faster, but it kept you from drawing attention to yourself if somebody happened to be walking by. Yes, keeping your cool was the most important thing you could do if you were going to boost cars. Trouble was, I always knew I had an honest face and that I would never be able to lie if I was caught. Jimmy was just the opposite. He didn't look so honest, and he could lie through his teeth and convince anyone if it was required to save his ass. I should have known I wasn't cut out for this when he got me to start boosting cars with him. But then, the money was flowing and, well, you can probably guess the rest.

That's what ultimately kept me involved … the money. At first, I have to admit there was a bit of a rush to it all. That feeling of hearing the engine start and then being behind the wheel of someone else's car. And, if we were lucky, someone else's nice car. I mean, eventually, we stole all kinds—everything from F150s to Jaguars. As long as there was a chop shop on the other end, we were going to get paid and paid well. Once I got the hang of it, well, it actually felt like easy money. Slide behind the wheel in the middle of the night, and it was a piece of cake.

Now, the chop shop was owned by T-Bone Williamson. He was a big man, and he always had the blues playing in his shop when we brought in the cars. Now, I was just learning about cars, but I knew a decent amount about the blues, or at least I thought I did. Well, right away, I noticed that T-Bone's name combined two great blues musicians—T-Bone Walker and Sonny Boy Williamson. That was pretty interesting, and I had half a mind to say something, but nobody spoke to T-Bone, at least nobody like us, unless we were spoken to.

T-Bone's place didn't look shady from the outside or the inside. It looked just like a garage, a very nice garage, with a full swath of mechanics under one roof and a fine collection of cars as well. Moreover, if you didn't know what you were looking for, you might go as far as to say it was classy, a high-class operation, and that's how T-Bone ran it.

At the same time, everyone knew that you didn't fuck with T-Bone. And you didn't joke with him either, since he wasn't known for having much of a sense of humor. Jimmy told me this straight away, and I was on guard from the first time I met him, only ever uttering the words "Yes, sir." T-Bone didn't have to say much either. He was just one of those men who imposed by his presence alone. But most of all, no matter what, you never crossed T-Bone. One guy named Bobby Higgins had decided to play ball with the cops some years back. T-Bone took care of that situation swiftly.

"What did T-Bone do," I asked.

"What did he do?" Jimmy repeated my question to me. "He sent Bobby down for the dirt nap … and quick I might add."

"No shit," I said.

"Real shit," said Jimmy. "Nobody messes with T-Bone."

The longer I went on running around stealing cars with Jimmy, two things began to change for me. The first was that stealing cars got easier and easier. I'd gotten over the anxiety I felt when I started, and I'd become a pretty good wheelman too. I managed to rationalize what we did and make my own excuses, and I was happy to be helping my family out with their finances. At the same time, I knew I'd gotten in with the wrong crowd. Not Jimmy. He was good people, even if he was a thief. But he was harmless. T-Bone was another story, and I knew that I should have gotten out of there long ago. But the longer I worked, the harder it was to leave.

~    ~    ~

Everything changed when I got pinched for stealing a car for T-Bone. I mean, nobody could have had worse luck than me. Nobody. Jimmy couldn't even believe it. I mean, what were the chances that I'd be boosting a car when an off-duty police officer was walking out of a pizza joint after a bachelor party? Fucking hell. Who does that happen to? Apparently me, and I was caught dead to right. The cops told me I was going to do some time unless I shed some light on the operation.

Well, that wasn't going to happen. Not in a million years. Because as scared as I was to go to prison, I was more scared of T-Bone. And it wasn't even close. The cops, of course, were disappointed. I was small-time. Beyond small-time. And they got nothing and no satisfaction from sending me to jail. Moreover, they couldn't understand why I would take the rap for T-Bone, but when they asked me, I just told them I liked breathing and off I went.

If you can believe it, my first visitor in prison was T-Bone himself. He was dressed nicely, in a silk button-down and dress slacks with polished leather shoes. He was smiling, and he'd brought me some magazines and books to read.

"Listen, kid," he said. "I just came by to see how you were doing and to say thanks."

I just nodded and smiled and said, "No problem."

"No, really," he said. "I appreciate it. When I first saw you, I have to admit I was suspicious, but you've got stones and, more importantly, loyalty. That's not easy to come by."

"Yes, sir," I said. "Thank you, sir."

"You don't need to call me sir," he said. "Call me T-Bone."

"OK," I said, before nodding. "Sir. T-Bone."

"That's more like it, kid," he said. "One more thing. I heard from Jimmy that you like the blues. Is that true?"

"Yes sir, I do," I said. "I love the blues."

"T-Bone," he said, correcting me. "Anyway, I put something together for you. It's an MP3 player loaded with the best prison blues of all time. I thought you might like to have it, at least while you're in here."

This was a surprise. I mean, here was T-Bone Williamson giving me a collection of the best prison blues just to help get me through my stay. I have no idea how he got this past the guards, but then I figured if anyone could, it would be T-Bone. This MP3 player had everything. I mean, it was a who's who of blues legends. I couldn't believe it. "Prisoner Blues" by George Clark. "Penitentiary Blues" by Blind Lemon Jefferson. "Prison Wall Blues" by the Cannon's Jug Stompers. "Jailhouse Blues" by Sleepy John Estes. "Death Cell Blues" by Blind Willie McTell. "Prison Bound" by Leroy Carr. It was a hell of a collection and one of the best gifts I'd ever received. I was touched, genuinely touched.

"Thanks," I said. "This is a hell of a gift."

"It was nothing," said T-Bone. "It was a hell of a thing you did for me."

I nodded, appreciative.

"Something to get you through," he said.

It seemed like the right time. It had to be the right time. I'd wanted to ask him this question for a long time, and this was as good a time as any for him to be receptive, receptive to me even when I was speaking without being spoken to. If not now, then never, right?

"So," I said. "I've got a question for you."

He looked at me quizzically and motioned, "Go on."

"Did your parents like the blues?" I asked.

"More than anything in the world," he said, revealing the only emotion I ever saw from him.

"Because—," I started but he cut me off.

"Because they named me T-Bone?"

"Yes," I said. "That's what I was thinking."

"Yes," he said. "That's why they named me T-Bone."

"Pretty cool to be named after, not one, but two of the greats," I remarked, in reference to Sonny Boy Williamson.

"It is pretty cool," said T-Bone. "I've never thought of it quite that way, but yes, it is."

"Anyway, thanks," I said. "I've always wanted to know."

"Why haven't you ever spoken up before?" he asked.

"Well, sir," I said. "With all due respect, you're a bit intimidating."

"Me?" he said, with all seriousness, before breaking out into laughter.

"That's funny, sir," I said. "Funny. But you get it."

T-Bone nodded and smiled and slapped me on the shoulder with his left hand while he shook my right.

"Enjoy the reading and the music," he said, then turned and walked out.

When I got out of jail, I was damaged goods, and no one wanted to hire me. That was OK, because T-Bone had taken care of my family while I'd been in jail, and he said he'd make a few calls for me. He couldn't promise anything, but he'd try, and that's how I got this job as a janitor. Head janitor actually.

I didn't see T-Bone for about six months or so, when he stopped by my job late in the evening, as I was cleaning up. I was wearing my headphones, and I didn't hear him sneak up behind me. He pulled the headphones off my head to have a listen. "Death Cell Blues" by Blind Willie McTell was playing.

"Good choice," he said, and I smiled. "By the way, how's the job going?"

"I got this, sir," I said. "Thank you. Thank you again. After all, it's not brain surgery."

I wasn't religious at all. Now, I'm not going to go as far as to say I'd shunned religion altogether, but I didn't believe in it. Not anymore. I wasn't even sure I believed in God, but I certainly didn't believe in religion, organized religion.

I'd grown up Catholic and, like so many others, I'd become disillusioned with the Church. Too many restrictions. Too many indiscretions. But most of all, too much despicable behavior by priests. One child molested was enough to break my faith, but the serial molestation that spread throughout the Catholic Church was as heinous a transgression as I could think of, and it destroyed whatever glimmer of faith I might have had left, way down deep.

My wife was just the opposite. Her faith was her backbone, the core of her being, and it was unending. And when it came to the Church's indiscretions, she didn't want to believe them, any of them. But when they were proven, she wanted the swiftest punishments imaginable for those men, even though she said she'd pray for them, along with their victims. However, when it came to the priest at our own church, my wife was adamant about his character. Their families had grown up together, and she had known him her entire life. He was the "the salt of the earth" and "as good as they come" according to her. She didn't have a doubt in her mind, and she went out of her way to tell me that "hearts broke" the day he decided to become a priest.

"He wasn't always a priest," she told me, which did little for me.

"None of them were," I replied cynically but practically.

Still, I had to admit that I liked Father Michael Murphy from the moment I met him. There are some people (not many, but some) who you can just trust implicitly, and he was one of them. I'm not even a trusting person, and I trusted him, not because he was a saint, but rather because he wasn't. He was humble and affable and disarming, and I knew I could rely on his character. Even a skeptic like me.

I suppose, in a roundabout way, I have to thank my wife. Without her, I'd never have considered going to church again. But church was important to her, and it was important to her that I go too, that I go with her, each and every Sunday. That's how I met Father Murphy, and that's how we became friends.

Unlike most priests, Father Murphy didn't focus all the attention of his sermons on God. Sure, his faith was ever-present, but so too was his faith in people. That seemed far rarer than having a strong faith in God. And despite his devotion to God, he never seemed to forget that we were all in the midst of a human experience, one that is dictated not merely by God, but by all that makes us human. I could identify with this, and it made his sermons more tolerable than any priest I'd ever listened to.

If I'm being perfectly honest, I didn't have many male friends, at least not as an adult. Not because I didn't get along with guys, but because I was married. Single guys hung out together, and married guys hung out with their wives, at least most of the time. That's just how it was. I'm not complaining. Not at all. But my wife made an exception for Father Murphy. Moreover, he wasn't really married or single. He was a priest or, as people liked to say, he was married to God. But I never believed that. At least, not completely.

Plus, Father Murphy couldn't really hang out in bars, at least not without attracting a lot of attention. And he liked to drink too. I mean, he might have been a man of the cloth, but he was also Irish. So, that wasn't going to fly in public, where he was likely to see a member of his parish. He drank like the Irish as well. Irish whiskey. Jameson. And he created a pretty good setup for himself in his office at the church.

If I am being fair, his office was more like a man cave than a religious space. Of course, it was complete with all the religious artifacts that any priest would have, but he also had a television. During the day, he'd use the TV for religious programming or even to show a member of his parish something inspirational. But, at night, that thing got all the cable channels, and he'd have the best games playing. Typical Irishman, he rooted for the Boston Celtics and Notre Dame, but he was a sports fan in general. I'd joke with him that he'd figured it out, figured out what all men were trying to achieve.

"You've got the perfect setup," I'd say.

"How's that?" he'd ask.

"Sports. Whiskey. No interruptions. Like I said, perfect."

"No women, either," he said.

"No women either," I repeated. "Like I said, perfect."

He laughed, natural and easy.

"That's right," he said sarcastically. "I planned it this way."

"Smart," I said. "You might start a movement."

"You know," he said. "It's not as if I don't like women. I'm still attracted to women."

This was one of the things I liked about Father Murphy that was different from other priests, hypocritical priests. Father Murphy was plum honest. Honest as it got. I could respect that, and I appreciated that he wasn't afraid to show that side of himself to me.

"That can't be easy," I said. "After all, there are some attractive, single women in your flock."

"It's not," he said plainly. "And there are, but I made a choice, and this is the choice I made."

"Do you ever wonder if you made the right choice?" I said.

"All the time. Don't you wonder about the choices you've made?"

"I do," I said. "I think that's only human."

"Exactly," said Father Murphy. "Priests are human too. And remember, we weren't always priests."

He laughed again and took a sip of whiskey.

"You and my wife keep reminding me," I said.

"I know what you're thinking?" he said.

"Oh, you do," I responded.

"You're wondering if I've ever broken my oaths," he said. "I have not. I made my choice."

"Well, you have all those cable channels," I joked, trying to lighten the mood. "Cinemax and all."

"Right," he said. "Who needs more than that?"

We sat there in his office drinking a bottle of Irish whiskey like a couple of regular guys. My wife didn't even mind it, because at least she knew where I was, in a church no less, with someone she could trust, so it worked out for everyone. Father Murphy enjoyed my company, and he knew I enjoyed his every bit as much.

"Do you ever get lonely?" I asked.

"Sometimes," said Father Murphy. "Just at night, really."

"Why's that?" I asked.

"Because that's when I'm alone. That's when the people have all gone home, the world is quiet, and the music stops."

"You ever listen to music, Father?" I asked. "Religious music? Irish music, perhaps?"

"I prefer the blues," he said, proudly. "Spin my records on that turntable over there."

"The blues?" I repeated. "Is that right?"

"You sound surprised," he inferred correctly. "Can a priest not listen to the blues?"

"I don't know," I said. "You tell me."

"What does that mean?" asked Father Murphy.

"Well," I said. "I would have thought the presence of the devil might have been a turnoff."

"Aah, yes, of course," he said. "Lucifer."

"Exactly," I said. "Many bluesman have evoked the devil. They've made deals with the devil. They've made friends with the devil. They've run from the devil. But the devil is always there."

"Yes, I suppose that's true," he said. "But the devil is there for all of us."

"Even you?" I asked.

"Of course," he answered. "Why wouldn't the devil be there for me. I am as human as anyone."

"I suppose," I said. "But aren't you closer to God than the rest of us?"

"All the more reason for the devil to pay me a visit," he said. "You know he likes a challenge."

"It seems like it would be a bad look for a priest to be cavorting with the devil."

"Who said anything about cavorting?" he answered. "Just because the devil's around, doesn't mean I have to listen to him."

"Some people say the blues are the devil's music."

"I am aware of that," said Father Murphy.

"But you still listen to it," I remarked. "Wouldn't that be frowned upon?"

"I imagine it would," said Father Murphy. "But why do you think they call the blues the devil's music?"

I stopped for a second and took a drink. This gave me time to think about his question. I felt pretty sure I knew why they called the blues the devil's music, but I wanted to be clear. I'd already alluded to the literal presence of the devil, so he must have been seeking an answer that went beyond merely his appearance in the songs.

"I suppose it has something to do with all the sins that are referenced in the blues," I said. "Lust. Greed. Murder. They're all there. And the lyrics can border on something that is less than pure as well."

"All true," he said. "All true. Everything you said is true."

"And still you're drawn to them," I remarked.

"Well, the blues do reference many sins," he said. "And they often center around the downtrodden and the poor, some of whom have sinned."

"Exactly," I said.

"But aren't they also worthy of our empathy and understanding?" Father Murphy asked. "Are their sins, so beautifully crafted through the blues, not equally worthy of God's forgiveness?"

"You tell me, Father," I asked.

"If the bluesmen I listen to, the bluesmen I love, are sinners, then the blues are their confession."

"Does that really qualify as a confession, Father?" I asked.

"For me, yes," he said. "I don't believe you have to come to church and sit in a booth to make a confession … or for God to hear you for that matter."

"That seems like a pretty modern interpretation, Father," I said.

"Well, I'm a modern priest," said Father Murphy.

"That you are, Father," I said. "I would agree with that."

Father Murphy walked over to his turntable. He reached down toward the shelf below and pulled out a record, which he carefully fixed on the platter. Then he moved the needle to the song of his choice. He took another swig of whiskey, as Skip James's "Devil Got My Woman" played over the record player.

"This is a good track," I remarked. "Well, at least you don't have to worry about the devil getting your woman."

"True," he laughed. "A silver lining."

"Little victories, Father," I said.

"Look, listening to the blues or songs about the devil doesn't mean the devil is inside me."

"Of course not," I say. "But the devil does seem to be in plenty of priests these days."

"You're referring to all of the scandals," he says, knowing that's exactly what I'm referring to.

"I am," I said.

"There are no words," said Father Murphy, visibly upset. "The devil may well be responsible, but the blues are not."

"Well, I certainly agree with you there," I said. "So, what can you do? As a priest, I mean."

"Unfortunately, not much," he said. "I can only continue to be the man I am. It's beyond my ability to reinstill trust in the Catholic Church, but perhaps I can maintain the trust in this one."

"You have, Father," I said. "I assure you that you have."

"What makes you so sure?" he asked.

"Because my wife is not easy to please," I said. "I am convinced there is no tougher critic."

"I've known her a long time," said Father Murphy. "That's high praise."

"You've earned it," I said. "Hell, I mean heck, she even lets me come here to drink and watch sports."

"I am glad she does," said Father Murphy.

"I bet you are," I said, joking. "After all, if your only company were murderers like Leadbelly and Blind Lemon Jefferson, there'd be no telling how you'd end up. Spending all your time listening to sinners like that."

"You mean instead of upstanding men like you who escape their wives and families to come drink whiskey in a priest's office."

"Touché," I said. "That hurt, Father. That really hurt."

He was a good guy, Father Murphy. He was a damn good guy, pardon my French. But I'm not sure he was joking, at least not entirely. And I'm not sure I was either, at least not entirely. I mean, I was, and I wasn't. After all, I held him to a high standard, being a priest and all, and I'd like to think he held me in similar regard. But I think we both knew that if we were sinners, our sins were minor. Now, I can't tell you who determines what is minor and what is not, but we weren't hurting a soul. We were just sitting back in a couple of swivel chairs drinking whiskey inside a priest's office. That's all. Overhead, the church bells struck twelve. Blind Willie McTell sang "Come on Around to My House Mama" and the night wore on.

When I was a kid, my sister listened to Whitney Houston a lot. One evening, my grandmother was over at our house when she heard the music coming from my sister's upstairs bedroom. She peered up the stairs, intrigued, before my father took her coat and hung it up in the front closet.

Then she peered up the stairs again before turning to me.

"Can you please fix me a drink, honey?" she said to me.

"Sure, Grandma," I said. "Scotch and soda?"

"You know it, darling," she said, proud that I knew her drink and could make it.

Now, I was only in high school at the time and well below drinking age. However, in our house, that didn't mean I was below drink fixing age, and Dad made sure I knew how to fix drinks for all the family members. Dad didn't even drink, but he said it was important to know how to fix drinks. In fact, he said it was more important to know how to fix drinks than it was to actually drink them. Anyway, he started us fixing drinks young and, by high school, I had become pretty good at it. Mom liked a vodka tonic. Grandma liked her scotch and soda. Aunt Belle always chose a Screwdriver and Uncle Wilbur drank his scotch neat. Always neat. So, yeah, I was a regular wizard around the small wet bar in our home.

My sister came downstairs to say hello just as I was returning with Grandma's drink.

"Hi, darling," she said, before peering up the stairs again. "Who's that singing?"

"Whitney Houston, Grandma," said my sister. "She's really famous."

"Oh yeah?" asked Grandma.

"Yes, she is," said my sister. "She's like, the biggest star in the world."

"I don't care if she's famous," said Grandma. "But she's not bad."

"Not bad?" interjected my mom. "Aretha says she's great."

"Aretha was better," said Grandma. "And Bessie Smith was better than both."

"Who?" I asked, as we walked into the den and sat down.

By now, we all had our drinks. Mom was armed with her vodka tonic. My dad was drinking a ginger ale, and my sister and I both had a Coca-Cola. Grandma sat down in the big queen chair in the room and was ready to hold court it seemed. I mean, she was old, but she was pretty cool, cooler than most grandmas anyways, always interested in what kids our age were doing without being quick to condemn. Still, she'd gotten pretty fired up about this conversation it seemed, and I didn't even know she listened to music.

"Did you just say, 'Who's Bessie Smith?'" she asked in relative disbelief.

"We've never heard of her, Grandma," I said.

"For crying out loud, Gerald," said Grandma looking at my dad. "Haven't you taught these kids anything?"

"I barely know anything about Bessie Smith myself," said my father. "Only that you and Dad talked about her from time to time. Oh, and also that Bob Dylan wrote a song about her."

Grandma just sat there shaking her head, almost like she'd failed as a parent. It was funny, but for the first time Grandma didn't look old. She looked young. Well, maybe not young, but she had a youthful attitude. Feisty. Energized. I could tell she was just getting started.

"Well, why do you think he wrote a song about her, you dumdum?" she asked before answering her own question. "Because she was great. Unimaginably great. Better than any Whitney Houston. No disrespect, honey."

"None taken, Grandma," said my sister.

"This Whitney Houston," said Grandma, "she sounds skinny. She sings skinny."

"She is skinny," said my sister.

"See!" said Grandma. "I knew it. She just sings from her head, her pretty little head and throat. Bessie Smith was a woman, a big woman, and she put her whole body into it. You felt the earth shake when Bessie Smith belted out a note."

"Mom," said my dad. "You can't tell a person's size from their voice. That's stereotyping."

"Was I right?" snapped Grandma.

"Yes, but—"

Grandma cut him off.

"But nothing, Gerald," said Grandma. "I can hear it. I can *feel* it."

We weren't sure what to say to that. Grandma was right, but we couldn't say things like that anymore. Nor could we judge people for those things either. But Grandma didn't know that. She didn't grow up that way, so it wasn't really her fault. Moreover, she hadn't been wrong about her inferences, and nobody was going to tell her she didn't have a point. At least, not if we didn't want to engage in another thirty minutes going toe to toe with the toughest old bird in Philly.

"What about Grandpa?" I asked. "Did he like her?"

"Of course," said Grandma. "He loved her. After all, she was progressive, contemporary, helped sexually liberate women at that time with her songs."

"Did Grandpa want a sexually liberated woman?" my mom piped in, smiling.

"Don't they all, dear," confided Grandma, with my dad sitting right there.

"This is uncomfortable," he said. "You're my mother."

"Not back then I wasn't," said Grandma emphatically, at which we all laughed except Dad.

"Where did you listen to Bessie Smith, Grandma?" asked my sister.

"Mostly on the radio, but there were some records too," she said.

"And you had a record player?" I asked.

"I didn't, but your grandfather did," she said. "And he'd put Bessie Smith on for us."

"Where'd you and Dad listen to her?" asked my father.

"In the parlor," said Grandma. "Back in those days, homes had parlors. That's where we'd sit together when we were listening to Bessie Smith … and necking."

My mom slapped the sofa between her and Grandma with her left hand and then placed it over her mouth laughing. Dad covered his eyes, and Grandma looked at him as if to say what was the big deal.

"What's necking?" asked my sister.

My dad hung his head lower. It was all too much for him.

"Making out," I whispered to her. "Or hooking up."

My sister giggled. This was officially the best family get-together we'd ever had. Dad walked into the other room and freshened Mom's drink when Grandma asked him to freshen hers as well.

"I think you've had plenty," said Dad.

"Hogwash," said Grandma. "Get me another."

"Grandma," I said. "Did you ever get to go to a show?"

"A show," Grandma repeated, uncertainly. "Oh, you mean, did I ever see her in person?"

"Yes," I said. "That's what I meant."

"Well, it wasn't like today with all these big tours," said Grandma. "But, yes, I saw her once, in 1930. Your grandfather took me."

"I never knew that," said my father.

"Well, you don't know everything," said Grandma.

"When were you planning to tell me?" asked my dad.

"Not sure I was," said Grandma. "I don't have to tell you. But since these kids are interested, I'll tell the story."

"Let's hear it," said my mom.

"Well," said Grandma. "There was a formal dance in town, and lots of young people our age were going.

One of those events where the young women wore evening gowns and the guys cleaned up well too. Ronnie Sanders had invited me to the dance, and I was planning to go with him."

"What about Grandpa?" asked my sister.

"Grandpa was sweet on me by then, but he hadn't made a move," said Grandma. "I was a good girl, but I wasn't going to wait around forever."

"So, what happened?" asked my mom.

"Well, eventually that slowpoke grandpa of yours got around to asking me to go with him," said Grandma. "I told him I would have loved to, but I had already told Ronnie Sanders I would go with him. Your grandpa just sighed, dejected."

"Oh no," said my sister. "Poor Grandpa."

"So, did you go to the dance with Ronnie Sanders?" my mom asked.

"I was planning on it," said Grandma. "But no, I didn't."

"And what about Bessie Smith?" I asked. "Was she playing at the dance?"

"Hell no," said Grandma, getting our attention. "The people who organized our dances were too square to ever have Bessie Smith there or even play her records. She was playing at the Orpheum Theater in Reading. This was 1930."

"Wow," said my mom.

"So, somehow your grandfather got two tickets, and he came back asking me if I wanted to go with him."

"What'd you do?" asked my sister.

"Well, of course I wanted to go with him," said Grandma. "And I might have wanted to see Bessie Smith even more."

"What about Ronnie Sanders?" asked my dad.

"You shouldn't be concerned about him," said Grandma. "Lucky for you, I didn't go to the dance."

"How'd you get out of it?" asked my mom.

"I stood him up," said Grandma. "Actually, I told him I was sick, a little white lie so he wouldn't feel too bad."

"This is unbelievable," I said.

"Unbelievable is right," said my dad. "What did you tell Gram and Gramps?"

"I told them I was going to the dance with your father," she said. "I dressed for the dance, and he did too. Then we went to the Orpheum."

"So, you lied to your parents?" asked Dad.

"I did," said Grandma. "They would never have let me go see Bessie Smith. Things were different in those days."

"What do you mean?" I said.

"Segregation?" asked my mom.

"You got it," said Grandma. "This was thirty years before civil rights."

"Did you ever tell your parents?" asked Dad, still hung up on that.

"Nope," said Grandma. "Your grandfather and I never did. They went to the grave never knowing. Didn't tell Ronnie Sanders either."

Grandma laughed. She laughed and she downed the rest of her drink. We laughed too and smiled and felt good. We felt good because Grandma had gotten to see Bessie Smith and because she had gone with Grandpa. And we felt good because she had told us. She had told us, as if she was telling the story for the first time, and perhaps she was. And she told us with the swagger of Bessie Smith, belting out notes, as if she was singing her own blues for all to hear. She might have been getting it off her chest, but we knew right then we'd never forget it.

After all, there are so few moments as a family that are revealing, truly revealing. You'd think they'd happen all the time, but the truth is, so often family members are playing a role, a role that has either something to do with their own age or the ages of other family members. And what this means is that multiple generations are rarely on equal footing, and this ended up being one of those rare exceptions.

For this brief time period, we were able to detach ourselves, at least my sister and I were able to detach ourselves. And we stopped seeing Mom and Dad as our parents and Grandma as our grandmother. They were just people, real people, who had lived real lives and had real experiences. People who had felt angst and joy and excitement, genuine excitement before the world had beaten them back down a little, the way it ultimately does to everyone. Because that's what happens. The world tears everyone down eventually, and someday it would tear us down too. But not that day. On that day, we listened to Grandma, and we heard the blues, Bessie Smith's blues. And nobody is old when they listen to the blues. Nobody. They are whatever age they want to be, or whatever age they were when they first heard them. In that way, the blues are like time travel. Grandma had brought 1930 into the present, and Bessie Smith had made it all possible. Grandma was old and older by the day. She wouldn't be around forever, and she knew this. However happy she was seeing us and sharing this story, deep down, everyone knows when death is near. She would pass away just a few months later.

"What was your favorite song?" I asked. "Your favorite Bessie Smith song."

"'Nobody Knows You When You're Down and Out,'" said Grandma, without hesitation.

Indeed.

The only thing Tommy Winston was afraid of was turning into his father. And that was a pretty big fear of his, even from a young age. We'd cast our lines into the river as teenagers, on a hot summer day, and it was nearly all he could talk about. Most guys talked about chasing girls, and Tommy liked girls too. But he was more worried about becoming his father. It consumed him.

Tommy's father was a bricklayer. He was a hell of a guy, and everybody liked him. Funny thing was, he didn't want Tommy to turn into him either. And the absolute last thing he wanted was for Tommy to become a bricklayer. In fact, he worked so hard and took so many jobs, in part, so he could be sure Tommy would have choices in life that he did not. It was admirable, and there wasn't a person in town whose respect Tommy's dad hadn't earned.

Of course, Tommy knew this and, deep down, I'm sure he admired it. But reality was different, particularly for a teenager. And it could get tiresome, damn tiresome, to hear everyone tell him just how terrific his father was, just how honorable his father was, everywhere he went. And not just honorable. He was likable. Whether it was at work, at the pub, or at home, Tommy's father was both someone you could trust and someone you could hang out with.

And he liked to hang out. In addition to being an adequate drinker, he could shoot a mean game of pool and was a pretty fair card player too. He was even a symbol of integration. You see, back then, the White people and Black people in our town rarely mixed. I wouldn't say there was actually too much racial tension, but you kept to your own and you hung out with your own. The geography of the town made this pretty easy to do, with most of the Black people living in one part of town and most of the White people in the other. All except for Tommy's father.

That's because bricks are color-blind, and Tommy's dad was good at laying bricks. Because of that, he handled a relatively equal amount of business in each part of town. And once you got to know Tommy's dad, well, he'd win anyone over. So, not only was Tommy's dad popular, but he was also the local do-gooder, bridging the gap between the Blacks and Whites.

Now, Tommy's dad wasn't trying to be a do-gooder. He wasn't looking for anyone's praise, and he certainly wasn't going out of his way to obtain the affection of the town. It just happened that way, partly because of his profession as a bricklayer and partly because he was a good guy. It was just the nature of the profession, and it suited his nature. One day, he'd be laying bricks for Mrs. Roth's garden in one part of town and the next he'd be stacking columns made of bricks in Mr. Johnson's yard in another part of town. He merely went where the business was, and since bricks were cheaper than other materials, his work crossed all demographic boundaries.

But billiards were different. He shot billiards, almost exclusively, in the Black part of town. And that was because that part of town was where all the best games were. It was where all the best billiard players played, and Tommy's dad frequented the halls there whenever he could. In all the years he went there, he never saw another White person in those pool halls. This was, in large part, because they weren't likely to be welcomed there, but also because most of them thought mixing like this was unnatural. Of course, they made an exception for Tommy's dad, the bricklayer, and he never thought twice about it.

He also liked the pool halls in that part of town because of the music they played. It was different than the music he listened to with his friends. Some of his friends listened to Black musicians, but not these Black musicians. They might have listened to Chuck Berry or Little Richard, but the pool hall played B.B. King, Freddie King, Albert King, Buddy Guy, and Junior Wells. They combined the blues of the South with Chicago blues, but it was all blues all the time at the pool hall. Tommy's dad didn't want to say much about the music for fear that he was trying too hard to fit in, that he might have been less than authentic. But he listened. He listened closely, and he heard something in those records that he had never heard before. They seemed to know him, understand him, empathize with him—the husband, the father, the bricklayer. He couldn't say it to anyone, but the music spoke to him in ways the music his friends listened to never could.

It also helped that Tommy's dad was a good billiards player. He was very good, and that always helps you earn respect. Add to the fact that he had done work for a number of the people who played there, and he fit right in. And when it came to Tommy's dad, the Black people in town were color-blind, much like the bricks he laid. Tommy's dad wished the White folks in town were the same.

So, Tommy and I would grab our fishing poles and head down to the river, pretty much any chance we got. I mentioned this earlier, but this wasn't just any river. This was the Mississippi River, the mighty Mississippi, which flowed with pace and power and had shores a mile wide. If you caught something big, that ole river could take you with it, so you had to be careful. But most of the time, Tommy and I weren't that interested in fishing, or at least our time wasn't defined by it. We were there to hang out, talk, and once we were teenagers, drink beer. That was enough, and if we happened to catch something, it was just an added bonus.

"You talk to Charlotte?" I asked.

Charlotte was the prettiest girl in school, and it was common knowledge that she had a crush on Tommy. She'd just broken up with her boyfriend, some meathead from the football team.

"You know I haven't," said Tommy. "Why do you always ask me that?"

"Because she has a crush on you," I said.

"So," said Tommy, unenthusiastically.

"So, any of us would lose our minds if she had a crush on us," I said. "And you just sit on your hands."

"I'm not you," said Tommy.

"I get it," I said. "But taking Charlotte out might do you some good. She's available, and she's a nice girl."

"She is," said Tommy. "But my mind is on other things, like getting admitted to college."

"I am sure you can afford to take Charlotte out and still get admitted to college," I said, with confidence.

"That may be true," said Tommy. "But I can't slip now."

"You won't," I said. "I'm sure of it."

"Listen," said Tommy. "You don't know what it's like."

I cast my line out into the water through some shadows that were creeping in.

"I don't know what what's like?" I asked.

"You don't know what it's like to be a bricklayer's son," he said. "And not just any bricklayer. *The* bricklayer."

"That's true," I said. "I don't."

"Most people misunderstand me, even you," he said.

"How so?" I asked.

"Well," he said. "You know I don't want to become my father, but do you know why?"

"Because you don't want to be a bricklayer?" I suggested.

"No," he said. "That's not it at all. I don't want to become my father because *he* doesn't want me to become him, and I respect him too much not to try and fulfill his wishes."

"Of you not following in his footsteps?" I asked, starting to get it now.

"Exactly," he said. "I've watched him all these years. I've seen him bust his ass, take jobs on the weekends. On holidays. I've seen it all, and I've seen him do it all, do it all for me, so that I could have a better life. That's a lot of pressure."

"So, it's not because he's damn near a folk hero in this town?" I asked point-blank.

"Well, that too," he said. "But I am proud of that. I'd be honored to try and live up to that."

I cast my line out into the water. The river seemed to be picking up speed as the day went on, but it was still hot as hell.

"Have you ever told him this?" I asked.

"Never," said Tommy. "I just say, 'Yes sir,' and let him know that my studies are going well, so that he knows I am honoring his wishes. He doesn't even know I love the blues."

"He doesn't even know you love the blues?" I asked. "Why wouldn't you tell him that? It would be something you could share together."

"Because that would make him worry more than ever," said Tommy. "Me telling him I liked the blues would get him thinking I wanted to be just like him."

"That seems like a shame," I said. "You could be a doctor and enjoy listening to the blues."

"I could," he said. "And maybe one day I will be, and then we can enjoy the blues together. But until then, it's not possible. I have to let him breathe, breathe easy. At least about this. He's worked hard enough."

"That's damn sad," I said.

"It is what it is," said Tommy. "But I owe him that. It's the least I can do."

"You owe him a detached relationship with his son?" I asked.

"In a way, yes I do," said Tommy. "I owe him the peace of mind that I am traveling on my own path, on a new path, on the path he's so desperately worked for all these years, in the hope that I would be something more, something more than he is."

Tommy went silent. He went back to casting, and I noticed he didn't even have any bait on his hook. He was just casting his line out, time after time, into the deep waters, hoping for I'm not sure what. Just casting, repeatedly, almost aimlessly, as the river swept by full of power, at its quickening pace. I had the sense that he was done, done talking and done with me. But something in me couldn't resist. It just seemed like there was more to say, even if he seemed perfectly happy to be casting his line out into the water, using a hook with no bait.

"You know," I said. "Your dad is a pretty remarkable guy. You said it yourself. People could do a whole hell of a lot worse than to be like him."

"Of course," said Tommy. "But not his son. He'd tell you there'd be nothing worse than for me to be like him. Nothing."

And that was it. That was the end of our conversation, our conversation at the river that day and our conversation about his dad. In fact, it was the last conversation we'd ever have about Tommy's fear of becoming his dad. We'd never talk about it, not like that, ever again. That's because that spring, Tommy's dad dropped dead of a heart attack. Just keeled over laying some bricks and was gone before the ambulance arrived.

That fall, Tommy dropped out of high school and started laying bricks. He had two younger brothers, and his mom needed the money. There wasn't anything to discuss, and Tommy simply did his best to fill his father's shoes. He inherited lots of clients and was able to bring in others. As for actually laying the bricks, he'd been watching his father for years despite his father's best efforts, and he knew what to do. He knew how the business worked and, most of all, he knew how to treat people. That was important, maybe the most important thing of all, and Tommy knew that. He knew that like the back of his hand, and people could sense his father inside him.

Although he wasn't nearly as good a billiards player as his father, he still stopped at the pool hall on the other side of town. He wasn't doing it to curry favor. In that regard, he was as authentic as his dad. No, he didn't want any special treatment at all. But he stopped into the pool hall because it was the only place in town that played the blues, the real blues, the blues he loved. From Charley

Patton to Muddy Waters. From the Mississippi Delta to Chicago. Riding the rails all across America, the blues played. And there wasn't anything Tommy liked more than the blues.

Funny thing was, Tommy Winston met his wife at the pool hall, when he dropped his money into the jukebox to play Jimmy Reed's song "You Got Me Dizzy." He looked up to see a woman standing there. "Do I?" she said.

"Well, that depends," said Tommy.

"On what?" she asked.

"That depends if you like the blues," he replied.

"I love the blues," she said.

"Well, in that case," said Tommy. "Yes, you've got me dizzy, but you must hear that a lot."

"Not from White boys," she said.

"I see," said Tommy.

"But I didn't say I minded it," she said. "What do you do?"

"I am a bricklayer," said Tommy. "A blues-loving bricklayer."

"I know," she said. "You think I don't know the only White boy in here? I know who you are."

"Then why'd you ask?" said Tommy.

"I wanted to know if *you* knew who you were," she said. "Seems you do."

"In that case," said Tommy. "Let's dance."

I don't see Tommy near as much as I used to, but I still see him from time to time.

I never wanted to go on that train trip. I couldn't understand it. We always flew on vacation but, for some reason, my parents had insisted we take the train that summer. That seemed like a terrible idea to me. My parents didn't care. They just said I'd have to make the best of it.

I tried to make the best of it. I really did. From the very first moment we got on the train, I tried. And I managed to make it a few hours before I started complaining, and that was only because the air-conditioning stopped working. What luck. Summer on a train. No AC. We lived in Chicago, and coming up from the South, it was hot. It was damn hot, and I could hardly stand it.

Normally, my parents were, at least, somewhat receptive to my pleas when I complained. But not this time. In fact, they were downright unsympathetic. I couldn't understand why. I mean, I'd complained about lesser things before and they'd listened. But they weren't having it. Not for a minute.

"You can read your new book," my mom said.

"Or you can stare out the window like we used to," my dad chimed in. "There's a lot of country out there you've never seen."

"A lot of nothing," I said, as we passed field after field. "There's nothing to look at."

"Nothing, huh?" snapped my father. "You hear that, honey? Nothing."

"Easy, dear," said my mother, trying to keep my father's blood pressure down.

"You heard him," said my father. "The boy said there's nothing out there."

"It's OK, honey," she said. "He's only sixteen."

"It's not OK," my father said. "Sixteen is old enough."

They were talking as if I wasn't there, which was annoying. It wasn't enough that we had to go on this godforsaken trip, but now they were acting as if I wasn't right next to them, even though every word was directed at me. Plus, they had quibbled about my age, with my father suggesting I was old enough to understand the meaning of this ill-advised journey. I was also old enough to do something else, and I couldn't resist. I knew I should've kept my mouth shut, but I opened it anyway.

"Old enough to drive too," I said. "Or fly. Which is what we should be doing. Instead, we're stuck here on a train with no air-conditioning."

"You hear that?" my father barked at my mother again, as if I wasn't there.

"Just try and calm down, dear," she said. "There's no reason to get excited."

"The hell there isn't," he retorted.

My dad was really a peaceful guy and pretty laid-back for the most part. I always felt like he was reasonable. Pragmatic. Logical. Usually, he was the calm one in the family. He'd take things in stride. But when he was pissed off, he'd let you know it. Fortunately, he didn't get pissed off very often. But when he did, he had strong opinions that he wasn't afraid to share. He'd dig in and fight if he'd been challenged, which is exactly what I had done. But now that I had gone this far, I decided I would keep going, see how far I could push him, try and understand what was really at the heart of his anger. I was sixteen, after all.

"What do you see?" I asked. "When you look out the window, what do you see?"

"I don't see nothing," he said, annoyed. "I'll tell you that."

"So, what do you see?" I repeated.

"Boys …," said my mother in hopes of diffusing the tension.

"I see fields," said my father. "I see crops in the fields. Fields where men worked in the hot sun, day after day, year after year. Men who made this country great. Men who made it free, who fought for what was right. I see land where troops once marched in the Civil War, land that was gobbled up and grew again."

This was one of those moments that was going to last, and I knew it. I could sense it. I could feel it. I was only sixteen, and it was true I thought I knew more than anyone else and certainly more than anyone else in this conversation. But I was also intuitive enough to see that this conversation meant something different to my father, that this conversation wasn't really one that was up for debate, or at least that this wasn't the time to debate it. I watched my father place his right hand over his eyes to conceal his emotion and then run his hand down his face toward his chin. My mom reached out and placed her hand gently on his back, and he took a deep breath while he looked down. Like I said, I was anything but humble, but this moment was an opportunity for me to be understanding, even if I was being understanding about things I didn't completely understand.

"You're right, Dad," I conceded. "That's not nothing."

My dad nodded, and my mom placed her other hand on my back, while Dad's head remained bowed.

"My boys," my mother said, smiling.

We kept to ourselves for the rest of the morning. I knew enough not to complain at this point, even though I was still wishing we'd flown or even taken a rental car. It was hot outside, and the sun flashed through the panes of glass and into the train car, which was already without air-conditioning.

I took the opportunity to look out the window and think about my parents and about what my father had said. It was easy for me to deduct that the scenery was less than scintillating, but it was also worth noting that this terrain, these landscapes, served people, allowed people to live and still did. The South was different. It wasn't like the logging towns of the West. The land here was different. It was fertile and wet, and it delivered cotton and tobacco and corn and wheat and rice. And it also brought us. The South was where our family originated from, and this was home before we went north and migrated to Chicago. No matter how dull it seemed, these were our origins and, if anything, I should have been grateful that someone in my family decided to leave these desolate fields and head north.

At lunch, the three of us went to eat in the dining car. We took the first available seating, in part because we were hungry, and in part because it was an opportunity to break the silence that sat between us after the somewhat painful resolution to our earlier conversation.

We were seated at a table for four. My mom and dad sat on one side, and I slid in all the way to the window on the booth bench across from them. After a few minutes, the waiter seated a man at our table to join us. That's how they did it on trains. They used every seat, and if you had open seats, they'd simply seat someone at your table. Speaking for myself, I was happy to have someone seated at our table because it meant the focus might be taken off me.

The man seated at our table was African American, slightly older than my dad, probably in his late fifties. He was lean and seemed to be in good shape, with only a small belly protruding. In fact, he might have looked even younger were it not for his completely gray beard that was cropped neatly and close to his face. He had a pleasant smile and was dressed far better than any of us, wearing a brown suit with a tie and sporting a stylish Stetson that he rested on the seat between us.

"Hello, folks," he said warmly. "I'm Delroy."

We all exchanged pleasantries with Delroy and welcomed him to our table. He was very calm and had a distinguished way about him. It also seemed like he sensed some of the tension between the three of us, and he sought to diffuse this immediately.

"Where y'all from?" he said, trying to break the ice.

"We're from Chicago," said my dad. "But my family is originally from Louisiana."

"Aah, the Bayou," said Delroy. "Always liked those parts. Good food and good music too."

"That's true," said my dad, making small talk while my mom and I sat quietly and looked on. "What about you, Delroy?"

"Mississippi's home for me," said Delroy. "Born and raised, and I'll die there too."

"Whereabouts?" asked my dad. "Not where are you going to die," he corrected himself. "Where in Mississippi are you from?"

"Tutwiler," said Delroy. "Just south of Clarksdale."

"Clarksdale," my dad responded enthusiastically. "Delta blues country."

"Those of us from Tutwiler would say Tutwiler is Delta blues country," said Delroy.

"But the Crossroads are in Clarksdale," confirmed my dad. "Yes?"

"Crossroads are everywhere," said Delroy. "We're all at a crossroads."

"Yes, of course," my dad said, smiling. "But Robert Johnson's Crossroads are in Clarksdale."

"That's true," said Delroy, taking a sip of his water. "You're right about that."

"That's what I meant," said my dad.

Delroy took another sip of water and then reached for his napkin, even though our food hadn't arrived. The napkin was folded neatly, and he snapped it out and laid it across his lap.

"I knew what you meant," Delroy said. "But the Delta blues were born in Tutwiler, long before Robert Johnson sold his soul to the devil at the Crossroads in Clarksdale."

"I didn't know that," my dad said humbly.

It was interesting, seeing my father humbled in this way. Earlier that morning, I had been humbled for my own naive conclusion, and here it seemed my dad was being humbled for his assertion about the blues. Now, his assertion was very common and less about naivety than ignorance. But one could argue that naivety and ignorance were more closely linked than it might have seemed. Still, it was interesting, interesting for me, and I studied my father's response, and Delroy as well, while they worked through the conversation. My mother, well, she was very protective of my father, and she sat quietly by his side, but I could feel her support.

"It's true, sir," said Delroy. "You know W. C. Handy?

"Sure," said my father.

"Well, it's been documented that he heard a man on a train platform as early as 1892 playing something that could only have been the blues," Delroy said, sharing his local knowledge. "Legend around those parts said it was a local field hand named Henry Sloan, but nobody can be sure. Either way, he was singing the blues more than three decades before Robert Johnson and the devil colluded. This is rarely talked about, but I'm sure you can imagine that us folks from Tutwiler take pride in these origins."

"Of course," said my father. "I imagine you would. Also, wasn't John Lee Hooker from Tutwiler?"

"Sure was," said Delroy. "Sonny Boy Williamson II as well. You know your blues, sir, or so it seems."

This could have come across as patronizing, since he had been the one giving my dad something of an education, but it didn't come across that way at all. I got the feeling it was genuine and compassionate and complimentary, despite his earlier correction of my father's comment.

"I try," said my dad. "Not as much as you, clearly. But I do love the blues, and our family has a connection with the blues as well."

This got everyone's attention, and I saw my mother lean in quizzically. After all, the three of us weren't particularly musical, and I'd never heard any stories about our family being linked to the blues. For a moment, I feared my father might be about to make something up in order to impress. But that wasn't his style. That wasn't his style at all, and it soon became clear when he started talking that he was merely sharing a story that none of us had ever heard before. I wondered why we hadn't, but it must have been true.

By now, our food had arrived, and we all started eating. However, once my father began telling the story,

Delroy slid his plate to the side, folded his hands on the table and leaned forward.

"I told you my family was from the South," began my dad.

"You did, sir," said Delroy, listening intently. "Yes, you did."

"But I didn't tell you why we left," my father said.

"No, you didn't," said Delroy.

"My great-grandfather was the one who settled in Chicago, but he wasn't so much moving north as running from the South," my father shared.

"Not sure I understand," said Delroy. "In those days, I thought only Black folks ran from the South."

"Upstanding Black folks and troublemaking White folks," corrected my father. "My great-grandfather was the latter."

"Is that right?" said Delroy.

Delroy seemed to have relaxed a bit and was now eating his lunch while my father continued. My mother and I were eating too, while listening, but my father had barely touched his plate.

"That's right," said my dad, not proudly. "Apparently, he was always in trouble. Nothing too terrible, mind you. Getting in bar fights. Some small-time thefts. And when he wasn't in trouble, he was chasing women, all kinds of women, which will get you in trouble too. He was basically wild, and he couldn't be tied down. Then he managed to sleep with a married woman, not knowing she was the wife of a prominent, local businessman. Well, that's just plain stupid, and it will get you killed down there, so he headed north. Only he couldn't very well buy a ticket, what with everyone from the authorities to the husband looking for him, so he started hopping trains. That was the safest way out, and he met a man named Bill Broonzy on his way to Chicago. And that's our connection to the blues."

"Big Bill Broonzy?" repeated Delroy. "You telling me your great-grandfather met Big Bill Broonzy on the way to Chicago?"

"That's what I'm telling you," said my father. "Only he wasn't Big Bill Broonzy then and he didn't play the guitar yet either. Apparently, he was a fiddle player. But great-grandad remembered his name when he made it in Chicago and became Big Bill Broonzy some years later. Even went to hear him play."

"That's quite a story," said Delroy. "Did your family start listening to the blues in Chicago?"

"Everyone listens to the blues in Chicago," declared my father. "It's a birthright."

"Even White folks?" asked Delroy.

"Especially White folks," said my father. "Or so it seems."

"Why do you think that is?" asked Delroy.

My father was eating his lunch now, having been unable to do so earlier while he was telling the story of his great-grandfather hopping trains.

"I'd like to think it's because the blues speak to everyone," said my father.

"You don't think it's because White people feel guilty?" asked Delroy.

"Guilty?" repeated my father, it seemed looking for clarification.

"Yes, guilty," he repeated. "For everything, or at least everything they did to Black people, beginning with slavery."

"Well, I don't know," said my father. "That's not why I listen to the blues."

"Not even subconsciously?" asked Delroy, pressing my father slightly.

"No," said my father, respectfully but firm. "I don't think so."

"Are you saying you don't feel guilty?" asked Delroy.

I looked at my mother, and she looked at me. Delroy was a perfect gentleman, but he was digging in pretty hard now. I wondered how my father would respond. He was a good man and a compassionate man. But he also wasn't the kind who was likely to tell someone what they wanted to hear if he didn't believe it.

"I feel badly," said my father. "In fact, I feel sick for what Black people in this country have had to endure. But I don't feel guilty. Not personally, anyway."

"Really?" said Delroy, surprised.

"Really," answered my father, unapologetically. "I don't believe it's my responsibility to shoulder the burden of the White man's actions any more than I think it's your responsibility to shoulder the burden of other Black men's actions."

"What does that mean?" asked Delroy. "What actions are you referring to?"

"All actions," said my father. "Good and bad. I believe we are only responsible for our own actions and should be judged accordingly."

"That's interesting," said Delroy. "I see your point. So, do you think I am judged for my actions in this country? Or do you think I am judged based on Black stereotypes?"

"Sadly, I'd guess you are often judged based upon Black stereotypes."

"But it's not fair for me to judge you based on White ones?" he asked.

"No, not really," answered my father, eerily poised. "It's not fair for either of us to be judged based on stereotypes."

"How about family?" asked Delroy. "Sins of the father and all that?"

"That seems more complex," said my father.

"Indeed," said Delroy. "I mean, if your family owned slaves, do you think you would feel guilty then?"

"Perhaps," said my father. "And if not guilt, certainly shame. I'd be ashamed of my family and my name. But my family didn't own slaves. We struggled from humble beginnings."

"I see," said Delroy. "But if you did, do you think guilt might be an appropriate sentiment."

"It might," said my father. "I would think so."

"So, perhaps some fans of the blues, those whose families might have owned slaves, could be listening out of guilt?" he asked.

"They could be," answered my father. "But I hope the music is the inspiration for their adulation."

"Nobody wants to be pitied," said Delroy. "That's for sure. Charity is worse than death for a proud man."

"I understand that," said my father.

"However, apology is something different," remarked Delroy. "As are reparations."

"So, reparations aren't seen as charity?" asked my father, interestingly.

"No," answered Delroy. "They're seen as a form of justice, far too late and not enough, but justice, nonetheless. A small step toward trying to balance the scales."

"I am all for balancing the scales," said my father. "But I'm not sure reparations balance out the scales or that there is anything that can be done to balance the scales or provide justice for terrible injustices."

"No?"

"No," answered my father. "And I worry that reparations are more like a payoff, and that White people believe they will absolve those who feel guilty. Or make those who feel terrible, like me, made to feel less terrible. And that doesn't seem right. We should feel terrible. Reparations or no reparations, history cannot be undone, and shameful acts are still shameful."

Delroy took a drink from his glass of water. He nodded, and he seemed satisfied by my father's answers. I sensed this wasn't the first time he'd had this conversation with a White man, but it was the first time he'd had this conversation with my father. My father was a White man, but he was his own man too. I looked at my mother and saw a look of relief in her eyes that the conversation had ended. My dad, on the other hand, never seemed to appear flustered, even if he had been very invested in the conversation.

"So, what's bringing you to Chicago?" asked my father, in an attempt to change the conversation in hopes that it might involve everyone at the table.

"I am visiting my son," said Delroy. "And my grandchildren."

"That's lovely," said my mother. "What does your son do?"

"He plays in a blues band," said Delroy. "Played with Buddy Guy for years. Imagine that."

"And you don't play music?" asked my dad.

"Not a lick," said Delroy.

"You didn't make a deal with the devil at the Crossroads?" asked my father.

"Nope," said Delroy. "Made a different deal, but one that didn't bless me with musical talent."

"Well, at least your son can play," joked my father. "My son's as tone-deaf as I am."

Delroy laughed. He had let go of the edge he displayed earlier in the conversation and returned to the warm, friendly tone he'd offered up when he sat down at the table. Actually, he'd never really lost his warm, friendly tone, even when he'd been engaged in that somewhat tense conversation with my father.

"You have a favorite Chicago bluesman?" he asked.

"Muddy Waters," said my father. "Hands down."

"He's from Mississippi too," said Delroy.

"I know," said my father. "Grew up near Clarksdale, where the blues were born."

For the first time, everyone at the table laughed. We laughed together, now that we had gone back, back to the beginning, the beginning of our conversation about where the blues had first begun. And we laughed without the need for anyone to add to the conversation, the need for anyone to be right or wrong or feel guilty. We just laughed, the way people laugh in the absence of hierarchy and history. Up ahead, we'd soon come to a railroad crossing, another crossroads. And there would certainly be more to come. But, for now, I just looked out the window, as floods of lush, green fields were blurred magnificently by the speed of the train as the light streamed in. It wasn't nothing. It was much more than nothing. It was something, I tell you, really something.

Sebastien was my best friend growing up. All through school, we were best friends. There weren't any other kids named Sebastien, at least not in our town. But his parents were French, and so they named him Sebastien. That was how he got his name.

For as long as I knew him, he'd gone by Seb, though. I think he went by Seb because it was easier to say, especially when we were kids. It was also easier to write, and he wrote Seb on all his papers. All of them that is except the ones he wrote in Mrs. Candell's English class, since she made him write out his whole name. I was never sure if she just wanted him to practice his cursive or if it was some kind of English teacher thing, more to do with formality and manners. Either way, he had to write out his whole name in Mrs. Candell's class, and she used his whole name when she called roll too.

In those days, I didn't think too deeply about my friendship with Seb, but knew I was lucky to have him. I knew enough to know that.

We lived close enough to school, elementary school, where we could walk together. And that's what we did. We walked together every day. We'd meet outside my house, which was just down the way from his, and walk there together. It made the day better to walk together, and Seb always had something interesting to talk about.

"Did you hear about the guy who robbed women's lingerie stores?" he asked.

I mean, it was always something with him, some obscure story or fact or some wild, hypothetical question.

"Did you know pigs don't sweat?" he asked one morning. "It's true, cool as cucumbers those pigs, even when they are about to be turned into bacon. Don't sweat at all."

I never knew where he got all this stuff, since this was in the days before the Internet, but Sebastien seemed to have an unlimited number of things we could talk about. This made our walks to school go quicker than they would have otherwise, and Sebastien always seemed to be in a good mood, even early in the morning, which was impressive to me.

Sebastien was a good-looking kid. Tall. Very tall. Taller than most. Dirty blond hair. Lean and athletic, even at a young age. As soon as girls started noticing boys, they noticed Sebastien. Plus, he had that French thing going on too, a touch of joie de vivre, only he didn't know it. That's what really separated him, set him apart from others, only he wasn't cocky at all. He was the opposite of arrogant, unassuming actually, and completely unaware and unaffected by his good looks and magnetism.

By the time we were ten, we were taking his little sister to school too. She was five years younger than Sebastien, with cute pigtails, a variety of dresses, and a porcelain white face that never smiled. In fact, if Sebastien could have been categorized as "happy-go-lucky" she seemed anything but. In fact, she was so quiet that, most of the time, I forgot she was even there. I mean, she didn't say a word. Not a single word. Not ever. And she just followed along, in step with us, perfectly behaved and yet nearly invisible.

The strangest thing about Sebastien's sister, though, was that he had never once mentioned her before he showed up with her one morning before school. In all our time together, on all our walks, he hadn't mentioned her once. That seemed incredibly odd to me, but when I asked him, he just shrugged it off casually and said, "I haven't? Oh, well, that's because she's quite a bit younger, as you can see." I left the conversation there, but that didn't seem like a reasonable answer. Or, perhaps the better way to say it would be that it seemed like an answer that was scripted rather than true. Either way, I let it go.

It also struck me as odd that Sebastien didn't make any attempts to change our conversations once he started bringing his sister along. And even when we started talking about girls, he seemed quite comfortable discussing these matters in front of her, even though she was so much younger. As always, she just tagged along, without saying a word, and she just walked into her classroom once we got to school.

By the time we got to high school, Sebastien was driving. He had an old Lincoln Continental that was pretty sweet. It was a great big car, and he loved driving it. He would arrive at my house with his younger sister in the car, and then we'd drop her off at her school on the way. She'd always get in the back seat when they arrived at my house, which I felt bad about. But she was already sitting back there by the time I came out of the house, and there was little I could do. At first, I tried to convince her to sit up front, but Sebastien told me to just give it up. For her part, she seemed very comfortable in the back seat, which wasn't so different from the way we'd walked to school, the three of us, when we were younger.

The best thing about Sebastien's car was that the car had a radio and a tape deck too. We listened to all kinds of music. Classic rock like The Beatles and The Rolling Stones. The Who. And, of course, Led Zeppelin. We turned it up loud, and it was the best part of my day.

"You listen to this stuff at home?" I asked.

"With my parents?" answered Sebastien.

"Sure," I said. "They must be cool, right? After all, they're French."

"Yes, they're French," he said. "But they aren't that cool. Maybe French cool."

"What's that mean?" I asked.

"They listen to a bunch of old French pop stars. Charles Aznavour. Francoise Hardy. Marie Laforêt. That kind of stuff."

"So, they don't get the Led out?" I asked, referring to the hour on the radio each night that played Led Zeppelin songs exclusively.

"No, they don't," he said.

"What about you?" I asked turning around to look at his sister.

Although she'd never spoken to me, I always felt bad that she was kept out of the conversation. Actually, I'd never heard her speak, but I still felt bad. Mind you, she never looked like she was upset about it. If anything, she might have seemed a bit relieved to be left out of our conversations. Most of them were dumb anyways, and she seemed quite comfortable just tagging along. Still, I'd tried to engage her from time to time. Sebastien would just tell me to forget it, but I couldn't. I couldn't forget it, mostly because it just seemed polite and, even when she tried to become invisible, I knew she was there. I knew she was right there. Walking. Sitting. Listening. Thinking. All the time. Right there.

"Hey, man," said Sebastien. "She's not going to talk to you."

"I know," I said. "But ..."

"Blues," she said from the back seat. "Blues. Only blues. I listen to the blues."

Sebastien just looked at me with surprise. Real surprise. He kept staring, and I told him to keep his eyes on the road so we wouldn't crash, but he just kept looking over at me, as if he'd seen something amazing. In a sense, he had. Of course, I had no idea how often she spoke at home, but she'd never spoken to me, to us, in all the time we'd been going to school together. Sebastien then turned his head all the way around, while still driving, and looked into the back seat. I did the same, elbowing him to turn back around. His sister was just sitting there, staring out the window, as a light rain streamed down the pane and onto the side of the car. She had returned back into herself, not saying a word, as she peered out the window into the wet street.

I thought about following up my question, but it was clear that she had disappeared again. She was gazing out, out the window, with a faraway look in her eyes.

When we got to her school, she opened the door and got out without saying a word, just the way she always did. She walked toward the building, and Sebastien said goodbye to no response from his sister. Sebastien just shook his head. I could tell he was still thinking about her response and the fact that she had responded to me at all. After she entered the school, he looked over at me and threw the car into drive while The Rolling Stones' "Tumbling Dice" played on the radio. Sebastien didn't say a word.

"And you said I should give it up," I said, smiling now. "After all these years of exchanging pleasantries."

"I don't know what to say," said Sebastien.

"Just say you were wrong," I joked.

"I was wrong," he said. "You can wear anyone down, even my sister."

"Come on, man," I said. "That didn't sound much like a compliment."

"I'm surprised," he said. "OK. I'm surprised."

"Thanks," I said, even though he wasn't exactly extending me a compliment now either.

I could tell that Sebastien wasn't just surprised by hearing his sister's response. He was shocked, almost troubled it seemed. And he'd made it very clear that he wasn't in the mood for my jokes or glib comments. It was as if things were OK, or at least held in check, when his sister was mute, day after day, week after week. But now, now that she had spoken for some unknown reason, it was almost as if the earth had been pulled off its axis. It was as if Sebastien's entire world had been turned upside down, or at least put off balance by a few simple words. I couldn't understand it.

Fortunately, for Sebastien, his sister went back to her previous silence. She retreated back into her own world in the back seat and, little by little, Sebastien returned to his normal self too. I don't think he had really been upset that she had spoken or upset that she had spoken to me. It was more like he was just startled, almost spooked, that his sister had broken her remarkable consistency, that she had abandoned her veil of silence for some reason. It wasn't really anything she had said or anything I had said. It was just unsettling, something so out of the ordinary.

Eventually, high school ended, and Sebastien went off to college on the East Coast. I stayed home here in Tulsa, which was fine by me. I worked a few different jobs—one as a bartender and another working the deli counter at the supermarket, until I finally found a steady gig changing oil at the filling station. I wouldn't go as far as to say it was a calling, but I liked it.

Sebastien and I tried to keep in touch, but it was hard to stay connected when he decided to go study in Paris for graduate school. When he was in college, at least he'd come home regularly, which meant we'd get to hang out on vacations and breaks throughout the year. One summer, we even went down to Mexico together for a week. But once he went to Paris, that became nearly impossible. Nothing had really happened to draw us apart. We had no falling out, or anything like that. It was just life, what life brings, and where it takes you that had changed things for us. And that was OK. That was more than OK. Sebastien's professional life had begun, and I was happy living in Tulsa and changing the oil at the filling station.

I suppose I must have been about twenty-six years old when a young woman pulled in driving a Lincoln Continental, and damn if it didn't look like the one Sebastien had driven back when we were in high school. The woman was wearing a black dress with a black leather jacket and a pair of black cowboy boots. She had red lipstick on and long hair that looked like it had been dyed black. I had never seen her before.

"This looks a lot like the car a friend of mine used to have," I said.

"Oh yeah," she said.

"Yeah," I said. "It was a pretty cool ride. Spent a lot of time in it."

"Is that right?" she said.

"Yeah," I said. "But he moved away. Anyway, just leave it here. You can wait inside. We have a waiting room, and it should only be about thirty minutes. Twenty, with any luck."

She grabbed her bag from the passenger seat, stepped out of the car, and walked toward the door that led to the waiting room.

I got in the driver's seat and pulled the car into the garage. This had to be the same car, Sebastien's car. I'd spent hours in his car, and I'd sat in it enough to know this was the same Lincoln, the very same Lincoln. Even the leather seats were worn in the same places. The next time I saw Sebastien I couldn't wait to tell him.

When I turned the key in the ignition, music came on, from that same tape player where we used to listen to our music. But this time it was Ma Rainey singing "Trust No Man." No way, I thought to myself. Not possible. No fucking way.

I finished up the oil change and walked into the waiting room to ring the woman up at the register.

"All finished," I said. "Checked your fluids too. Everything's fine."

"Thanks," she said, while she pulled cash out of her bag to pay for the oil change. "I told you I liked the blues. Don't you remember?"

It was hard to believe this was reality, that she was reality, that she was Sebastien's little sister. There was simply no resemblance to the young girl who had sat in the back seat of that car. None whatsoever. She was all grown up. No pigtails. Dark hair. Leather. Cowboy boots. Just hardened. Tougher, even though she seemed pretty tough back then too.

"Of course, I remember," I said, smiling.

"Listen, if you ever want to grab a drink, I work at Cain's Ballroom," she said. "You know the place?"

"I do," I said. "An institution in this town. A blues institution, too."

"Imagine that," she said, as she took her keys from my hand and walked toward her car.

~ ~ ~

About a week later, I decided to stop by Cain's Ballroom around closing time. She was wiping down the bar, wearing a tight white top and jeans, with her hair pulled back. I was still pretty shy and not all that confident with women, unlike her brother Sebastien. But I was happy to see her and, as far as I could tell, she looked happy to see me too. Or at least not unhappy. I suppose, as happy as I could imagine her being is a better way to put it.

"You hungry?" she said. "Because I'm hungry."

"Sure," I said.

"Good," she said. "Just give me a minute to finish up."

She completed her duties behind the bar and then called out to a man, who must have been her boss.

"Hey, Earl," she said. "I'm taking off."

She didn't wait for a response, grabbed her leather jacket, and walked out from behind the bar.

"You feel like waffles?" I asked.

"Waffle House?" she asked.

"Is there any other?" I replied.

"You really know how to treat a lady," she said in a voice that was mildly sarcastic. But she smiled, so I wasn't too worried.

We were seated in a booth at the far end of the restaurant. She ordered waffles, bacon, hash browns, along with steak and eggs, while I just ordered a side of waffles and a coffee.

"You weren't kidding," I said, upon seeing her order.

"Do I look like a kidder?" she deadpanned, making me think both about her now and in those younger years when she looked serious as could be on our walks to school and in the back seat of Sebastien's car.

"No, you do not," I said.

"Precisely," she replied, letting me know she hadn't exactly become verbose even though she was speaking now.

The Waffle House was starting to fill up. Even at this late hour, it was filling up, probably because other people had just gotten off work. Add to that the insomniacs and the partyers who had just left the clubs and, well, you've got a decent crowd pretty quickly. She seemed to like the noise, as it made it harder to talk or easier not to—depending on how you were looking at it. I wasn't sure, but it seemed like she was going to tell me something before it got louder. However, the infusion of people also seemed to come as a relief, or at least she seemed to welcome a moment to organize her thoughts.

The food arrived quickly, and we dug in. She actually ate faster than I did, and she really was starving by the manner in which she attacked those waffles, which were soaked in syrup and butter, before moving on to the rest of her food.

"So good," she said, with her mouth half full.

"Never disappoints," I added. "Not many things in life you can say that about."

"True," she said. "So true."

We smiled at one another in agreement and kept eating until our plates were clean.

"I'm sorry," I said.

"What for?" she asked.

"For always trying to talk to you when you were younger," I said. "I must have been annoying."

"You weren't," she said.

"Well," I said, "I could see your brother's response that one time you answered. He wasn't comfortable with it at all, and it made me feel bad."

"You shouldn't," she said. "Not at all."

"Well, I think it made things a little weird with him," I said. "At least for a while."

"Don't feel bad," she said. "You were always nice to me. Funny too."

"Alright," I said. "Thanks for making me feel better."

"Anytime," she smiled.

The waitress came over, and I asked Sebastien's sister if she wanted to get a chocolate sundae.

"They're pretty good here," I said.

"Why not?" she answered, smiling.

"Great," I said.

Then she leaned forward across the table as if she was going to tell me something. It seemed like something important by the way she moved, and then she sat back as if she might be having second thoughts. Only she wasn't having second thoughts. She was just relocating, and she slid out of her side of the booth before sliding in right next to me. She then placed her hand on my chest as if feeling for my heart and leaned her face against my shoulder, almost nuzzling it, with real affection.

"Don't look at me," she said. "Please. Just listen."

"OK," I said, slightly afraid but listening.

"So, Sebastien never told you?" she asked.

"No," I said, shaking my head, assuming whatever she was about to share had never been told to me.

"Our house," she said, beginning to softly whimper against my arm. "Our house was a terrible place."

"What do you mean?" I asked, without looking at her as instructed.

"The worst kind of terrible," she said. "The very worst kind. My father … my father, our father was a monster. He was the worst kind of monster. The very worst kind. I was just a little girl."

In the horror of her confession, I hardly knew what to say or if to say anything at all, so I said the only inadequate words that came into my head, the first words that came into my head.

"I'm sorry," I said. "I am so sorry."

"The blues," she said. "That's why the blues. That's why I listened to the blues. The strong, resilient women who sang the blues like Bessie Smith and Ma Rainey, Billie Holiday, and Memphis Minnie. That's where I went. That's where I disappeared to and never came out, swore I'd never come out. Ever again. Thank God I had the blues. The blues and Sebastien were all I had."

"What about your mother?" I whispered.

"Afraid," she said. "Just afraid of that monster. But Sebastien put an end to it. One night, once he was bigger than my father, he put an end to it. He beat my father within an inch of his life and put a knife to his throat. Told him he wouldn't be so generous if he ever touched me again. And then it was over. I just kept listening to the blues and didn't say a word. I came and went, in my own world, with the blues in my head and my eyes open. I got into the car and got out, went into the classroom and left, went home and went to bed and got up in the morning. Until I left home for good."

By this time, I had wrapped my arm around her, and she was crying harder now. I pulled her closer and placed my lips against her jet-black hair that was stuck to the side of her head. I placed my lips there and kept them there, for a long time it seemed, until I took them away and placed them there again.

"Where are your parents now?" I asked.

"He's dead. Fucking dead. I might have killed him myself had he not had a heart attack and gotten off easy. My mother is in a home, an assisted living facility, where she just stares out the window blankly all day long, they say from PTSD. I say from guilt, but either way."

We hadn't touched the chocolate sundae, which had now melted into a sort of swirled smoothie. She was still sitting next to me, holding on tight, and she had asked me not to move, if that was alright with me, which of course it was.

I no longer wondered why Sebastien had looked so surprised that day when she had answered me in the car. It was all so clear now, so incredibly clear. Part of me wished he had confided in me, but part of me was glad he hadn't. After all, how do you talk about the unimaginable? How do you speak about the unspeakable when there are no words?

Just like there were no words for Sebastien's sister. No words for what had happened. No words for what she'd endured, and what she would always have to live with. There were no words, not really. No words then and no words now. So, we just sat there, with the liquid sundae in front of us, the sounds of the Waffle House reverberating, and the grease wafting in and out across our noses in our own self-imposed, somehow beautiful silence. We stayed like that, just like that, while music played in the restaurant. Billie Holiday's "Lady Sings the Blues" came on.

"I love this song," she said. "When it's over, take me home. Take me home and hold me. We can put on some music, but please take me home. To your place."

Alton was a hell of a lawyer. Hell of a fuckin' lawyer I tell you. One of the best. The best around, which is why it was such a surprise when he just gave it all up. And when I say he gave it up, I mean he gave it up. This wasn't simply the case of a guy switching firms or moving from the prosecution to the defense. I mean this guy just walked out the door, picked up his briefcase and left. Never even returned to clean up his office. To be honest, it was a little fucking eerie, particularly for the rest of us who still worked there. But that's what he did. That's exactly what he did.

I'd been friends with Alton ever since I joined the firm. In some ways, he was like a mentor to me. If not a mentor, he was something to aspire to. I mean, he had it all. Big house. Sports cars. Vacation home. Traveled the world with his beautiful wife. And did it all in style. In fucking style, that guy. Everything was top shelf. The clothes. The watches. The shoes. The scotch. And why not? If you can do it, why not? As far as I was concerned, he was living the life, the goddamn boss life, the life we all aspired to obtain someday.

So when I walked by his office in the days following his departure, it was quite a shock. Not just that he was gone, but the way he left things. The only thing I can compare it to is when someone dies suddenly. Only Alton wasn't dead. He was very much alive, alive as the rest of us, only different. He had seemed to go from caring more than anyone to not caring at all. At least about this shit. This shit in his office. This legal shit. And he did it overnight. Over fucking night. And he was gone, gone for good, just like that.

Of course, I tried to call him, but he had disconnected his phone. So, I called his house. His wife answered the phone, and she told me he had left her too and that he had taken off. Traveling, she said, even though she had no idea where he'd gone. Left everything but his blues records, she told me.

He really had fallen off the grid. Or perhaps walked off it. But it wasn't like he had just changed his number. He'd disconnected his phone and turned it back in. Apparently, he felt no need for it. No need to be connected to the world. No need to be connected to his world. To *our* world. No need to be connected to anyone else. Or anything else. Just out there all alone, ramblin' along. To this day, I still can't decide if I think it was the most selfish thing I'd ever seen or the most inspiring. Maybe both.

But Alton did what seemed impossible, for any of us to do, after so many years on earth. He disappeared. Literally vanished. Nobody heard a thing about him, which seemed inconceivable, since he had been an important man, with important ties, who knew many important people. And yet, somehow, he had done it, pulled off the impossible. He was nowhere. Nowhere at all. And nowhere to be found.

Of course, this improbable disappearing act only fueled more sensational rumors. The most prevalent was that he was just living the good life in London or Paris or maybe on a beach in Tahiti. That he had only left his job, this job, without abandoning the life. Without disposing of all the expensive things, all the niceties. Dining in top-drawer restaurants in some fantastic city or lying on the white sands in an exotic location with only blue water ahead. Those rumors actually made us feel better in some strange way, not just about Alton, but also about ourselves. After all, what the hell were we working for, working so damn hard for, if it wasn't the good life?

You'd think the most awful rumors would be the ones about Alton being dead, perhaps in some daring quest through the Amazon Rainforest or downed in the Congo on a dangerous expedition. But those rumors, however terrible, were still more in line with what we all saw as a spectacular life, a dynamic existence. And although we cringed at the thought of something bad happening to Alton, there was glory in the idea of such a fantastic conclusion.

As you might expect, there were the outlandish rumors too. Like the one that said he joined a circus or the one that opined he was playing professional poker in Macau under the name Vincent Tanino. One rumor even got started that he was working as a spy for the US government in the Middle East. There was simply no end to these rumors and the longer Alton was unaccounted for, the more they grew.

However, the most disconcerting rumors were the ones that invalidated our own lives, the ones that made us question our own existence. Those were the ones that were downright terrifying, and I tried not to think about them. Because, if Alton had come to the conclusion that this life, this life we had all chosen, was ultimately meaningless, well … what did that say about us? Was it simply meaningless for him rather than meaningless in and of itself? Or did it deserve greater contemplation?

The idea that we'd all been wasting our time, the precious time we had, was almost too much to endure. But if Alton had ultimately come to that conclusion, we'd have to find some way to justify our own choices.

It was a few years after Alton had disappeared when I ran into Alton's wife at an event in Midtown Manhattan. She was there as the guest of another lawyer, and she looked as smashing as ever. I'd gotten to know her a little bit over the years, and I liked her. Mostly, I liked her because she never pretended to be anything but who she was. And she liked fancy parties, fine clothes, and all the luxury she could experience. There was no pretense about her pretentiousness, and I admired that. I'd also thought she and Alton were a match made in heaven. When she saw me, she excused herself from her date and walked over to say hello.

"It's good to see you," I said.

"You too," she answered. "It's been a while."

"Three years," I said. "Just before your husband left the firm."

"Ex-husband," she corrected me.

"You're divorced now?" I asked.

"Nearly three years now," she said. "I'm told it was the fastest divorce on record."

"Divorces are never fast," I said. "Particularly when the assets are considerable."

"This one was," she said. "Alton gave me everything."

"Everything?" I repeated.

"Everything," she said, almost as surprised as I was it seemed. "We split the cash and he gave me everything else. Both houses. Both cars. The boat in the Hamptons too. Stocks. And every material possession we owned with the exception of those records he took, and what did I care about the blues anyway? His records. They were the only thing he took. He gave me everything. Literally everything."

"Just like that?" I said.

"Just like that," she said. "Haven't seen him since or heard from him since."

"Neither has the firm," I said. "Not a word."

"You think he's OK?" I asked.

"I don't know," she said. "And caring does me little good, so I try not to care. You'd would be wise to do the same."

She was right. Of course, she was right. Alton had made his choices, whatever his reasons. And Alton had cut his ties. Cut his ties with us. He had cut his ties and, apparently, never looked back. And yet here I was still asking about him, wondering about him, at times even worrying about him. It was counterproductive to keep thinking about him. I knew it, and I still kept doing it. I think it was because I just couldn't get my head around what he had done, and I wanted to know why. Of course, I'd heard of midlife crisis before—some guy going out and buying a sports car or doing a triathlon or even dating a woman half his age. But this was different. This was sheer abandonment of every aspect of his life, and I would be lying if I said I didn't feel abandoned too. Maybe it wasn't so much that I had been abandoned. After all, Alton bore no responsibility to me. Not personally anyway. But it was more like my life's choices had been abandoned, almost like I'd been traveling along a long, strenuous highway with someone, and they just decided to get off. That felt like its own form of abandonment.

Eventually, though, I forgot about Alton. Or at least became less obsessed with his disappearance. I still remained curious, of course, but all of my leads had dried up. No one had seen him in many years, and so I suppose I had given up any hope of finding out what happened to him.

That was OK. It had to be OK, really, in order for my own life to move on. And my life had moved on. I'd made partner at the firm and gotten married. We had two small children, and we'd bought a nice house in Westchester County. Things were good for me, very good, and I couldn't complain. Not at all. I was happy.

~     ~     ~

We'd had a conference in Nashville for the week. It was pretty standard fare, as far as conferences go, but it was fine. It was perfectly fine. Some of the younger attorneys were staying the weekend in Nashville, but that held little appeal for me. I was older now, and besides, I was married with two kids as well. Normally, I would have just headed home, but my wife was spending the weekend at her mother's place in Rhode Island. So, I had a couple days to myself, and my wife told me to enjoy them. Rather than stay in Nashville, I decided to drive to Memphis.

I'd never been to Memphis, and I'd always wanted to go there. Obviously, Graceland held some fascination, but I really wanted to go to Beale Street and listen to some blues. I only started listening to the blues after Alton had left the firm. I am not really sure why, but I think it was because I just couldn't get it out of my head that the only thing he took with him were his blues records. Of all the luxurious things he owned, all he valued enough to keep were those records. That was startling, and it set me on my own path of trying to discover the blues. I started with the Delta blues singers, but I'd fallen in love with B.B. King.

Everything about B.B. King had struck a chord with me: that wailing guitar he'd named Lucille, his commanding voice, and his live performances that only expanded upon his records. Even his prodigious size was appealing, in that it commanded a certain level of respect, of gravitas, that reminded you that you were in the presence of something greater than yourself, much greater than yourself. In any case, B.B. King had a blues club on Beale Street in Memphis, and that seemed like as good a place to go as any. There were blues clubs up and down Beale Street, and I was excited to get away and listen to some music. It seemed like the perfect weekend getaway after a week of meetings and conferences.

So, I hopped in my rental car and headed out for Memphis at the conclusion of our meetings on Friday morning. I was struck by the green desolation and long swaths of farmland as I drove between these two cities. It was a nice spring day, without a cloud in the sky, and the sun was shining. It was just beginning to heat up, and I could only imagine that summers here must get pretty hot. For now, though, it was perfect.

After a couple hours, I pulled over to get some gas. I filled up the tank only to realize that it was one of those exits that didn't allow you to get back on the freeway, at least not right there. This always annoyed me, and I wondered why anyone would ever construct an exit with this design. Fortunately, I was in no hurry, and I just followed the signs along a pretty scenic access road that almost split the fields in two on the way back to the freeway. It was pretty, damn pretty, and I was almost glad for the inconvenience. Up ahead, I saw a sign for some fresh fruit along the side of the road, and I decided to pull over, since I had left in a hurry before lunchtime.

There was a small stand along the side of the road with apples, grapes, blackberries, lemons, and other items that all looked good. And there was a man wearing a cowboy hat, sitting in the back of an old Chevy pickup truck, playing an acoustic guitar, with his legs swinging off the end. He was probably in his mid-fifties, strong and lean, with long hair that was predominantly grey and a close-cropped goatee. I pulled my car over, and he half-nodded without really looking up, while he continued to strum his guitar, playing what appeared to me a pretty impressive riff from Robert Johnson's "Love in Vain." I stepped out of the car and made my selection.

The man set his guitar on the ground and leaned the neck up against the back gate of the truck. Then he hopped off, if I am being honest, like what appeared to be a much younger man. He was wearing jeans and a white T-shirt with some cowboy boots. As I was picking over the fruits, I could feel him walking toward me, closer and closer, almost uncomfortably close, until he was just a couple feet away. So, I turned to ask him to give me some space only to see Alton staring back at me.

"Fucking hell," I said, as I dropped my bag, spilling the fruit across the dusty ground.

Alton just stood there smiling, shaking his head and smiling, grinning really, from ear to ear while I stood there not knowing what to say next. He put his hand out and said, "It's good to see you. Really. It's damn good to see you."

I shook his hand, and he pulled me close and gave me a hug like a brother might. I'm quite certain that Alton had never hugged me before, but he hugged me now. It might have kept me from falling over, the shock being so great it almost made my knees weak. He patted me on the back a couple of times and then stepped back to look at me, while I looked back at him.

Alton had deep blue, inset eyes I would have recognized anywhere. But, other than that, he had transformed his physical appearance. Gone were the Armani suits, replaced with the wardrobe you might have found on a ranch hand. He had also let his hair grow out, along with his tidy goatee. But the biggest change was his body. He must have dropped forty pounds from the last time I saw him. I would never have categorized him as fat, but he had grown a bit paunchy like most of us do when our lives become more sedentary, the expensive meals are served, and the drinks flow. Alton had been the prototype for that lifestyle, and his physique had displayed all those characteristics. However, the guy standing in front of me didn't have an ounce of fat on him. I might have described him as wiry, but he was clearly strong, and I even noticed the muscles in his forearms rippling when we shook hands. It was strange. His face looked older, weathered and sun-worn, but his body had returned to the body of a young man. It was stunning.

"Let me give you a hand," he said, as he bent down on one knee to pick up the fruit I had dropped.

"Thanks," I said, still trying to get a handle on the magnitude of this unlikely moment.

"Here you go," he said, handing me the fruit as if I was just another customer.

"Alton," I said. "I ... I don't know where to begin. I just can't believe it."

"We can begin right here," he said. "Right here in the heart of Tennessee, about fifty miles from Memphis."

"Alright," I said, not knowing what else to say.

"You got time for one beer?" he said. "Know you're driving, but one beer won't hurt you."

"Sure," I said.

Alton walked over to his truck and reached into the back of the flatbed, where he had a cooler. He grabbed a couple of Tecates out of the cooler and tossed me a can. Then he hopped back onto the gate of the truck, with his beer in his hand and his legs hanging over the edge. He just stared at me, smiling naturally, while the sun beat down on our heads. He slid his cowboy hat over, while he wiped his brow and cracked his beer open. He looked like the freest man on earth, and I had honestly never seen him look so happy.

I had it in my mind to sit next to him, except I worried about my suit getting dirty if I hopped up onto the truck. Alton picked up on this and said, "That's a nice suit, man."

"Thanks," I said, slightly embarrassed at my desire to keep it clean.

Alton just sat there drinking his beer, maybe waiting for me to say something. I stood across from him drinking mine, with a thousand thoughts rushing through my head from all the way back to the day he left up until this moment. It was just such a surreal thing to be here, in the heart of Tennessee, drinking beers in the afternoon sun with this man who had been my friend, my colleague, and who had disappeared off the face of the earth more than a decade ago. I was almost in a trance. But Alton slapped my shoulder to snap me out of it.

"Well, how you been?" he asked, genuine and without a hint of judgment. "Still at the firm?"

It was funny. In some ways, he was exactly the same. Warm and personable and charming as ever. He just had a natural charisma that always made people feel good, feel at ease, and this was one of the things that had made him such a great lawyer. At the same time, he had never seemed so totally at ease with himself. I mean, it was honestly disarming to see him appearing so comfortable, as if a hundred tons of baggage had been lifted off his shoulders since the last time I saw him. The Alton I had known was ferociously ambitious, while the man in front of me looked completely content, as if he had not a single thing to prove. If anything, it almost made him seem more powerful, sitting there in jeans with a beer in his hand and his legs dangling off the side of an old pickup like the freest man I had ever laid eyes on.

"I'm good," I said. "Real good. Still at the firm. Even made partner."

"That's great," said Alton, seeming genuinely happy for me. "Married?"

"I am," I said. "To a great woman, and we have two great kids."

"That-a-boy," he said, like a real cowboy but a cowboy who was cheering for me. "I'm happy for you. Really happy for you."

If Alton was anything, he was sincere. He was always sincere, and I always appreciated it.

"What are you doing here?" asked Alton. "I mean, what brings you here."

"I could ask you the same thing," I said, and Alton laughed.

"That's funny," he said. "And true. But come on, man, what brings you to these parts?"

"Conference in Nashville," I said. "My wife has the kids at her mother's for the weekend, so I decided to head to Memphis and listen to some blues."

"Goddamn," said Alton. "Good for you. When did you start listening to the blues?"

"After you left," I said. "I called your home looking for you, and your wife told me you left everything but your blues records. Figured there must have been some reason you took them with you."

He nodded like he was almost proud of me. But Alton had always been one of my supporters.

"So, did you figure it out?" he asked.

"Figure what out?" I asked. "Why you left?"

"No," he said, laughing. "Did you figure out why I took those blues records with me."

"Because they're fucking great," I answered excitedly, with the most unsophisticated answer possible. After all, I didn't know shit about the blues, but I knew I liked them.

"They are great," said Alton, who seemed to get a kick out of my answer. "No better companion out there than the blues. You have a favorite?"

"B.B. King," I said. "*Live at the Regal* is my favorite album of all time."

He smiled again, and he just kept smiling, as he tipped his beer back and finished it off. It was something really. I had never seen him so happy, so damn happy, as he looked in the back of that truck. He shook his head and nodded and then shook it again, still smiling.

"There's hope for you yet," he said warmly. "Actually, there was always hope for you. I always knew things would work out for you, and I'm glad they did."

All of the questions had focused on me, when I had so many questions for him. After all, I wasn't doing much different from the last time he saw me. Sure, I'd gotten married and started a family, but I was traveling along the same path, unlike Alton who had vanished from our lives overnight and disappeared into an abyss. Apparently, this abyss. Anyway, this seemed like the right time to turn the tables and try and understand what happened, what had happened to Alton.

"What happened?" I asked.

"What do you mean?" he said.

"What happened to you?" I repeated with clarification. "And why did you leave? Why did you leave like that?"

"That's history, man," he said. "Do you really want to talk about that?"

"Actually, yes," I said. "It's all I thought about for months, maybe years."

"Really?" he said, appearing surprised for the first time since I ran into him.

"Yes," I said. "Look, I'm just glad you're OK, and I am happy to see you. Really happy to see you. But … yes."

"Alright," said Alton. "It ain't no secret. I got nothing to hide. Why don't you come round for dinner tomorrow and we can catch up? I'll whip something up for us. I got a place outside of Memphis. Bit of a drive, but it's a nice spot."

"Great," I said.

Alton reached inside his pocket for a piece of paper, then asked if I had a pen, which I did. He wrote down his address on the paper and told me I'd have to figure out how to get there, since I wouldn't be able to call him because he didn't have a phone.

"No phone?" I said. "Landline or cell?"

"Nope," he said smiling, as if it was a real accomplishment, which it actually was. "Not for me."

I extended my hand, and Alton jumped off the back of the truck again and took it. He pulled me close one more time and gave me a big hug, then dusted me off to be sure he hadn't dirtied my suit too much. Then he walked me over to my car, kicking the dirt coolly with his boots.

"See you tomorrow," I said, as I buckled up.

"Drive safe," said Alton, before slapping his hand on the roof of the car above the driver's side window.

I drove the rest of the way and checked into the hotel in Memphis. I had picked a place strategically, so that I'd be close to Beale Street and the blues clubs. I decided I would grab a bite at the clubs and headed over to B.B. King's joint, where I ordered a burger that wasn't half bad.

This was the first time I had ever heard the blues performed live. I can't even remember the name of the musician, but he wasn't anyone famous. Still, he was very good, and I enjoyed watching him and the other players perform. I think what I enjoyed most was the manner in which the compositions unfolded and what seemed like a sort of life of their own they took on as they were played. The band members spoke conversationally with the audience between numbers but, during the songs, they almost seemed to forget we were there, as the music and their own interplay swept them off to someplace else. In such a small venue, sitting near the stage, this was visible, and I was struck by how engrossed they seemed to be with their experience, their own experience of playing, of performing. Sure, they were playing for us, but it really did seem to mean something to them, something personal, independent of our presence. That was very different from any other music I'd seen performed live, and it was exciting to witness in person.

The next day, I slept in late and grabbed brunch at the hotel. I don't think I had realized how exhausted I had been from the day before—what with the conclusion of the conference, drive, Alton, and the night out on Beale Street. But I really was wiped out. After lunch, I walked around town for an hour or so, before I returned to my hotel room and decided to watch some TV before heading out to Alton's place. I didn't really know what to expect. Did he have his own family? What was his life like? His home? I'd looked up the address on Google Maps, and it looked like he lived in the middle of nowhere. It was one of those addresses, that couldn't actually be found on Google Maps, where they give you an address nearby to map to, but at least I had an idea of where he was and how to get there.

It took me about an hour to drive to Alton's, with most of the roads small and narrow once I had exited the freeway. We had picked a time when it was still light, which made it easier, and thank goodness I could put the location into my phone, since I would never have believed this was correct without digital confirmation.

When the map told me I had arrived, I was still on the road, but there was a gravel drive close by, and I drove down it. At the end of the drive there was a silver Airstream, parked on what appeared to be many acres of land all stretched out ahead. Alton was outside, waiting for me, with the grill already fired up and a couple of dogs running through the green fields behind him. He took off his cowboy hat and waved me in.

Alton was dressed eerily similar to the day before with jeans and a T-shirt and the very same boots. The only difference was that he now had a plaid, flannel shirt over his T-shirt that hung loosely and remained unbuttoned. I parked the car and got out wearing the most casual clothes I had, which were slacks and a polo.

"Welcome," shouted Alton, as he walked over to greet me. "This is my place."

"Thanks," I said. "It's beautiful out here."

"I like it," said Alton. "Suits me."

Alton handed me a beer and let me know it would be about a half hour until the steaks were ready. He had some baked potatoes too, and I have to admit it smelled good. I'd never known Alton to cook back in the day, but he seemed to be getting around the grill pretty well. He had a couple of chairs, like the ones you see parents sit on at kids' soccer games, that were set out in front of the Airstream. We sat down across the plaid patterns on the chairs as the sun began its slow descent from the sky.

"How much land do you have?" I asked.

"Just under eighty acres," said Alston.

"Are you shitting me?" I asked.

"I'm not," he said. "Grow those fruits and vegetables on it too. It's a little bit of work, but I enjoy it."

"That's your job?" I ask.

"It is," he said. "Just work hard enough to make what I need to live, which isn't much. Pay for my food, gas, the dogs' food. That's about it. Plenty of time left to do other things, other things I want to do."

"Fuck me," I said, still stunned by Alton's transformation. "And you sleep in there?"

"You mean the Airstream?" he laughed. "Yes, I sleep in there."

"I'm sorry," I said. "It's just … it's just so hard to believe. Maybe not believe, but understand, at least based on knowing you as a corporate lawyer in your previous life, in your old life with me."

"It's fine," he said. "I get it. Believe me, I get it. I never expected anyone to understand or tried to get anyone to understand or even cared if anyone understood if I am being perfectly honest."

"Obviously," I said. "Since you didn't tell anyone."

"Listen," he said. "I didn't have to tell anyone. It was my business. Everyone always feels like they have a right to other people's business, but they don't. I told the firm I was leaving. I took care of my wife. And I didn't owe anyone else anything."

"I'm sorry," I said. "You're right. You're absolutely right. You didn't."

Alton walked over to check on the steaks. They were almost ready. He called the dogs over and gave them each a small piece of meat. Then he tossed a stick into the field for them to chase.

"Only a few more minutes," he said. "Let me show you my place."

Alton turned and walked toward the door of the Airstream. He opened the door for me to step up and enter. The inside of the Airstream was clean, very clean. Immaculate really. He had a bed, small sofa, desk and a table, but it didn't feel cluttered. Not at all. On the table was his record player, and his records were lined up underneath. The Airstream included a small kitchenette and a bathroom as well. But it was striking how organized and tidy the place was. I mean, there wasn't anything out of place, which may have made it feel bigger than it was. It certainly felt bigger than it looked from the outside.

"Place is neater than your office was," I said.

"That may be," he said. "Not surprising, really. I have less stuff now."

"Definitely less paper," I said. "That's for sure."

"It is," said Alton. "Don't miss that. All I need now is one file drawer for my fruit business, tax documents, and so on. Simpler."

We walked back outside, and Alton took the steaks and potatoes off the grill. He dished them up on sturdy picnic plates and grabbed a couple of stack tables for us to use in front of our foldout chairs. And we sat there, just the two of us, eating some pretty damn good steaks, with beers in our hands, and green as far as the eye could see as the sun plunged beneath the horizon. In its own way, it was amazing, a sort of paradise really, but it was also such a long way away from the city. It was a long way away from the life Alton once led, and it didn't resemble my life in Westchester in any way at all. In fact, it was so far removed that it was almost beyond comprehension, and I am not sure I would have believed anyone lived like this had I not seen it for my own eyes.

Even so, the fact that Alton lived like this, that he lived like this by choice, was still hard to get my head around. But I was glad to be there, and I was glad to have run into him. I was glad to know he was OK and that he was alive. Those feelings were strong and palpable.

"So, you want to know why I left the law?" he asked.

"Yes, that's part of it," I answered. "And the life. And why you did it the way you did it."

"A three-part question, huh?" he said, chuckling a bit but very calm, relaxed even. "Sure, I get it."

"I do want to know, but you don't have to tell me," I said. "I understand that."

"Like I said yesterday, it ain't no secret, especially after all this time," he said.

"Alright," I said.

"You ever have days when you don't want to be a lawyer anymore?" he asked.

"Of course," I said. "It can be a grind and, at times, a crisis of conscience too."

"Exactly," said Alton. "So, what do you do when you have those days?" he asked.

"I suppose I try to just get through them," I said. "Survive and move on."

"I did too," said Alton. "Until those days were more frequent. Then I wanted more than to just *survive*. I wanted to *live*."

"So, you just quit?" I asked, even though I knew the answer.

"You know I did," said Alton.

"Well," I said. "You can't just quit."

"That's the thing," said Alton. "You can."

"But what about the stigma?" I said. "What other people will think."

"Who cares what other people think?" said Alton.

"I care," I said. "And I think most people care."

"Well, then that's a problem," said Alton. "Because most people will look down on you. It's the only way they can justify their own lives, by beating on you, on your decision, by pushing you down beneath them, and you can be sure they'll do it every chance they get."

"I would think that would be tough to face," I said.

"That's why you can't let yourself care what they think," said Alton. "But facing that isn't as tough as living a life you don't want to live. At least not for me."

"And what about all the time you'd already put in?" I asked. "The time you put in to get there. LSATs. Law school. The bar."

"So," said Alton plainly.

"So, that's a lot of time," I said.

"So," said Alton. "Are you saying that, since it took a long time to get there, you should spend the rest of your time unhappy being there?"

"That's not what I'm saying," I said. "Well, maybe a little bit. I am just saying you have to wonder what the time was worth if you leave the law."

"I don't think you do," said Alton. "The time was worth whatever it was worth, whether you stay or go. You've no control over the time spent. But you have total control of how you spend the remaining time you have left. People who choose to be unhappy deserve to be unhappy."

"Are you saying I deserve to be unhappy?" I asked, feeling slightly offended.

"Not at all, man," he said. "Unless you are unhappy. And I don't know if you are unhappy or not.

You said you were happy, so that's great. I can't tell anyone else how they should live their life. That's not for me to say."

"And the way you did it?" I asked.

"Only way, man, I'm afraid," said Alton. "Sorry about that."

"What do you mean?" I asked.

"No offense, but I didn't need anyone's permission," he said. "And I didn't want anyone's advice."

"I understand that," I said.

"Then you'll understand the way I did it was the only way, man," he said. "Everyone's got an opinion. And everyone wants to give you their advice, which is usually self-motivated anyway. Plus, I don't need anyone calling me about a client or an old case. No thanks, man. But you are forgetting the most important part about all of this, this whole deal. There's one thing you haven't thought about, haven't asked about, and it's the most important factor of all."

"What's that?" I asked, feeling dumb enough already for whatever I'd overlooked.

"Everyone assumes I was running away from the law when I left it," he said.

"Well," I said. "Weren't you?"

"In a sense, yes, and you could see it that way," he said. "But it was more about what I was running toward than what I was running from. That's what this was all about."

"OK," I said. "So, all your life, you wanted to sell fruit and live in a trailer. That was the dream."

"It's funny, man," he said. "I would have thought you were smarter, but if that's what you see, if that's all you see, then yeah, that's it. You got it. You figured me out."

The moment I said it, I knew I shouldn't have. I knew it right away, even before I said it, but I just couldn't help it, couldn't help myself, and it made me realize I was just like all the rest. I was just like everyone else in the office, settled into our lawyerly lives, closed-minded, thinking we had it all figured out. Thinking we were better. That's who I was and, hard as I tried, that part of me had become hardwired, much as I wished it wasn't. And perhaps, deep down, I was just hurt, on a personal level that is, that he hadn't told me or reached out to me. Either way, I had acted like a jerk, like the petty fools Alton knew we were. I had proved his point right then and there, and he knew it. It might have hurt some people, but I don't think it hurt Alton. Not at this point, anyway. In fact, I think he gained a certain satisfaction from me proving his own point without him having to argue it, almost as if I had played into his hands.

"I'm sorry," I said. "It's just hard to understand."

"But why do you care so much?" he said. "Why do you even care?"

It was utterly embarrassing, but I had to tell him the truth at this point. He knew the truth. He'd always known it, but he was just waiting to hear me say it. He'd been waiting to hear me say it from the first moment we started talking, and now I'd have to.

"I guess I'm just worried, deep down, that your life is better than mine," I said. "I think that's what everyone worries about, that someone else's life is better than our own. I think that's why we just want everyone to fall in line with our decisions of conformity?"

"Do you know how fucked-up that is?" said Alton.

"I do," I said. "It sounds horrible, like I'm horrible. But I'm just being honest."

"I know you are, man, and I appreciate it," he said. "But with all due respect, this is your problem, not mine. This is your fucking problem."

Alton stepped inside the Airstream and reappeared with a bottle of whiskey and two glasses.

"I'm driving," I said.

Alton poured the two glasses anyway and placed one in front of me.

"You're welcome to sleep on my sofa," he said. "But suit yourself."

"Alright," I said. "Appreciate it."

We sat and drank whiskey outside in the Tennessee air, while the dogs lay at our feet. Alton played his guitar a bit, and he was good, damn good. He had learned how to play the blues, and he did it as unpretentiously as everything else but no less well. We were outside, while he played. The night was clear, and we could see the stars. Alton started a fire, and we stayed up drinking and talking for hours, like old friends, better friends than we were when we worked together as lawyers too. Much as I might not have wanted to admit it, Alton belonged here, as much if not more than he belonged in a courtroom, no matter how good he was. This place suited him, and everything about him said that. He wanted to look at the land when he woke up each morning, play the blues on his guitar for hours on end, and listen to his blues records at night. He wanted to work with his hands and earn just enough money to live his life but not a cent more. He wanted to watch the sun come up and watch it go down, and not from some "damn office building" he said. This was home. This was his home, and by the end of the night the only thing I was sad about was what he had to go through to get here, what anyone had to go through if they didn't want to conform. That was a shame, the real shame in all this.

Conformists like me simply weren't cut out to step off the path, to go against the grain, to defy norms. We just weren't built like that. And where Alton had to carve his own path to obtain happiness, I was happiest staying on the one that had been carved out for me. I couldn't have survived out there for a week, and yet here was Alton, tan and fit and living like someone out of a goddamn Clint Eastwood movie. The truth was that if I told people at the firm that Alton lived on eighty acres of beautiful land, played guitar most of the day, spun his blues records, cooked steaks under the stars and worked as little as he wanted, every one of them would have been jealous. And yet, I can't think of a single one who could've survived out there, would have wanted to survive out there, on the land, in an Airstream, without their Range Rovers and Porsches and gated communities and flights in first class. Not a single one. That was the real irony. But Alton could, and I envied him, even if I knew I could never be him.

The next morning, we woke up in the afternoon. That's what Alton said. I'd never heard that, but I liked it, and I told him I might use it sometime. But it had been one of those nights that turned into day. Anyway, when we finally got up, Alton made a damn good breakfast out on the grill—bacon, eggs, sausages, potatoes, grilled onions, peppers, the works.

"You working today?" I asked.

"Sure," he said.

"What time do you start?" I asked, laughing at the absurdity of it all.

"Whenever you get on the road," he said, laughing. "And not a minute before."

"I expect nothing less," I said, and he nodded.

"So, what are you going to tell them at the office?" asked Alton. "I mean, when you get back."

"Just that the blues flow from every corner of Memphis," I said. "From the Beale Street musicians to fruit vendors on the side of the road. Then they'll ask me what I mean, and I'll tell them that it's difficult to explain. They'll just have to go and see for themselves."

David Joseph is a recipient of *The Paul Cave Prize for Literature, Next Generation Indie Book Award*, and other honors. He is the author of four collections of short fiction, and his writing has been published in *The Wall Street Journal, London Magazine, The Smart Set, Litro*, and *Rattle*. A recipient of The John Henry Hobart Fellowship for Ethics and Social Justice, he has taught at Pepperdine University and Harvard University, where he received The Derek Bok Award For Distinction in Teaching. In 2024, Readers Digest named his book *I Didn't Know What To Say, So I Just Said Thanks* as one of the 38 Best Short Story Collections of All-Time.